THE CROWN IS MINE

Takeover Season

Part I

THE CROWN IS MINE

Takeover Season

Part I

Warren Holloway
Good2Go Publishing

Table of Contents

Chapter 1

HARRISBURG, PENNSYLVANIA; PRESENT DAY

"You mutha fuckas counted me out, like a this ain't my city!" Tracy 'TK' King said, after kicking in the door on a nigga's crib he was clocking since his release last week, after serving ten years for having to shoot a nigga for trying to burn him out of a kilo of cocaine he fronted him. TK having his twin black steel 9mm Berettas in hand, aimed at the main target along with this young goon standing firm with his AK-47 drapped off his shoulder. Those in the room knowing who TK is, wasn't aware that he was even home or heard that he was suppose to be coming home. Especially with someone of his previous hood status. TK standing five foot ten, black colored eyes adding to his dark stare, dark skin, close cut with a bald fade on the sides, goatee that's looking sharp. TK a husky nigga from all the push ups, pull ups, dips, and lifting that steel in the yard. He fell when he was twenty, now he's thirty still holding on to his youthful thugged out look. TK is also holding a grudge on anyone who didn't hold him down or tried to shit on his name when he was down, like he had the L. His main focus now, is to reclaim his position of power and respect as it once was. "This is a new day and a new time nigga. This shit ain't how it was when you was home". Big Butch aka B-Mor said puffing on the blunt, blowing out a cloud of smoke in TK's direction. TK didn't come for small talk or disrespect. He fired on the two goons by Big Butch dropping them with head shots, then shifting his weapon on Big Butch, firing a gut shot on his fat ass, weighing close to three hundred pounds, dreadlocks, full black beard, gold teeth with diamonds in them. "Aggh nigga! You going die for that shit!" Big Butch snapped in pain, turning to his young teen soldier with the AK-47. "Shoot that mutha fucka!" TK locked eyes with the young nigga seeing he's gripping the handle of the AK-47. The young thug didn't want to risk being put down, so he waited, standing firm not wanting to move, gritting his teeth. Big Butch holding his stomach that's spewing blood from the hot molting slug that tore through his flesh. The two females on the couch, sitting there on their phones. "Put them mutha fucking phones down, before I shoot them out of your hands!" TK said firmly jolting the females, making them toss the phones on the coffee table. At the same time when TK turned to address the females, the young teen goon tried to raise the AK-47 up to take TK out, until he caught the fast movement out the corner of his eye, firing rapid

8

The Crown Is Mine

rounds on the little nigga, slugs slamming into his chest piercing his lungs. "That little nigga had some balls trying to get at me". TK said now aiming both guns at Big Butch, who is staring back at him intently, wanting to kill him where he stood. "I know that look, don't worry, no more witnesses or mistakes. Now give me what I came for". TK said. Big Butch worked up a hulk spit, knowing there is no way out of this situation, so why give up the money or product easy. He spit in TK's face. " Fuck you nigga, get that shit that hard way. Dead or alive I run this shit!" Big Butch snapped, standing his ground. TK calmly looking over at the women on the couch who's showing fear and confusion, not knowing if they should try to run or sit and wait until he kills them. TK wiped the spit from his face onto Big Butch's Gucci shirt, before taking one of his 9mm Berettas placing it underneath Big Butch's chin. "No, fuck you nigga!" TK said pulling the trigger, startling the females as Big Butch's brains leaped out the top of his head spraying out chunks of skull and flesh. "I'll take over from here". TK said standing, making his way over to the females. " Where he keep his money and work?" "There's money under the mattress in the bedroom". The first female volunteered. "We just dropped a duffle bag of bricks off. He put them in the kitchen". The other female added. Each of them hoping to be spared.

"You, go get the bag of bricks. You, go up and get the money. Leave your phones here". TK directed the two light skinned females. The first returning quick with the cocaine. " It's thirty bricks in there, twenty he got on consignment". The female said. "Yeah he ain't gotta worry about that debt anymore. That shit was cleared when I put bullet in his head". TK slightly being humored by his own words, feeling the power of this beginning stages of his take over. " You going to kill us?" The female asked only nineteen, standing five foot even, thick with curves in all the right places, hugging the light blue denim jeans with her DKNY pink shirt that's filled by her perky 36C breast. TK becoming serious looking on at her honey brown eyes displaying fear. The fear that the life she wants to live out is about to be canceled like the rest of these mutha fuckas inside this house. Plus she heard him say; No more witnesses or mistakes. "What's your name?" "Sugar Baby, cause I be getting spoiled out here". She responded, his eyes shifting towards the steps, wondering what's taking this bitch so long up there? He did have plans on killing them, not wanting to leave no witnesses. Now this chick is trying to soften him and his approach, with her looks and calm tone of voice. Something he isn't use to, being in the hard environment of state prison for ten years. " Come on, your girl probably need our help with the money". TK said. He let Suga Baby go up the steps first with her fat curvaceous ass staring back at him. He shook his head, wishing he would have met her under different circumstances. Not like this, while he's in beast mode, trying to take his position at the top, supplying the city. "Tati! What's taking you so long bitch?" Suga Baby said calling out to Tatiana, the five foot five filled out beauty with a mole on her upper lip, right side, adding to her sex appeal. Light grey eyes, hair dyed blond in two braids that reach her ass and wide hips.

Tati being the outspoken feisty one of the two, always quick to think or react in situations like this. Also not one for allowing her being a female to be a reason to be disrespected. Soon as they entered the room, seeing the mattress flipped up with a large sum of money still present, the rest gone, just as Tati is not in the room, the window wide open, showing her escape. Suga Baby knowing how crazy her girl is, gave off a light laughter. This angered TK even more. "You think this shit is a fucking game!? I will leave you here with the rest of them mutha fuckas downstairs!" He said pressing his gun to her forehead. Her heart racing just as fast as her mind trying to find a way out. Then it came to her, as her survival instincts kicked in, wanting to live. "She can't get far. Her phone is downstairs, plus I'm the one that drove us over here". Suga Baby said quickly. TK now knowing he can't kill her. He needs her to help track her girlfriend, before she runs her mouth alerting the city to his presence. " Come on, we going to get the phones. You take the bag of bricks the way you came in. What kind of whip you got?" He asked so he know what direction to walk in once out side of the house. "Panamera Porsche". She responded grabbing the phones, securing the bag. They exited the crib walking to the candy apple red Panamera with the chrome package, 23inch Lexoni rims, TVs in th headrest, with the PS5 game console for her baby brother when he rides with her. The plush tan leather and Bose system, all concealed behind the dark tinted windows. TK was wearing his shades and Nike hat flowing with the all black attire, T-shirt, jeans and black Nike Airmax. " Let's go find this crazy bitch, before she make this shit worst than what it is". TK said. Suga Baby now thinking of the reality of this situation, her girl Tati could have gotten her killed, if TK thought otherwise. They drove for a few blocks, before Suga Baby spotted Tati limping carrying the bag of money.

Tati having jumped out of the second floor window with the bag of money fearing for her life, plus thinking about the come up at he same time, running with the money. When she seen Suga Baby's car, she figured she made it out alive, she got excited coming over to the car. The passenger window came down revealing TK's pissed off looking face, along with his 9mm Berretta pointing at her. She couldn't turn and run, with her body still shocked by the hard landing, even with her adrenaline rushing through her body, she didn't want to be shot by

The Crown Is Mine

this crazy nigga. "Get the fuck in the car before I leave you standing right there". TK said firmly staring at her with dark murderous eyes. She got into the back seat having a attitude. " Now what? We got the money and drugs for you? Take it and let us leave, me and my home girl we don't know shit and we ain't see shit". Tati said knowing she can't outrun or over power him. Suga Baby also looking at TK wanting to know what he's going to do with them. "Letting you go is not an option, so you either ride with me putting work in, or we can end this conversation right now". TK responded. His gun aimed at Suga Baby, while checking in the back seat to see Tati's face awaiting their responses. "Okay, how much of this money do we get for riding with you? " Tati fired back agreeing with TK. "Y'all can split all of it. I'll take the thirty bricks and flip it". " You for real it's like a half a mil up in this bitch?" Tati asked, not expecting that response from him. "It's the price of your silence and loyalty. Now let's focus back on my next move". " What's your next move?" Suga Baby asked. "To be king of the city, running shit like I use to". "It's different than it was before you went to jail". Tati said. "I keep hearing that like I give a fuck. If I did you wouldn't be sitting back there with a half a mil". He said leaving them with that thought, as she drove off blasting OWED TO ME; By Trav, French Montana and Jim Jones...

Chapter 2

"Aye Four-Five, look at this shit on Fox news". Tony 'T-Black' Black said turning the volume up as he tuned in to the shooting in the South Acres projects of the city. The reporter standing outside of the home. "This two story home is the graphic crime scene of what police are saying was a robbery homicide. With the victims all being known drug dealers who caught the worst end of this life of crime. Detectives are saying these homicide cases are usually open and shut, when they follow the trail of money. In which they left behind what they couldn't take from the looks of it detectives stated. The victims three adults and one minor, most of them armed got gunned down unable to use their weapons. This is tragic for the city and families of these victims". The brown skin female reporter said before showing footage of the inside of the house. Four-Five and T-Black knowing who's crib that was hit. They didn't fuck with B-Mor like that, but didn't hate on him getting money either. "How that shit jump off when he be with a squad all the time?" T-Black said. T-Black a short nigga standing five foot seven, skinny built with a big heart, not standing down for anyone. He did a bid when he was sixteen for shooting at the cops, sending slugs through their cars when they chased him. Now twenty six and a half, he's still about that street life, getting money and staying loyal to the nigga that held him down when he was locked up. Demitrius 'Four-Five' Carter, a boss of the city, moving bricks on the low, having started in the hood on the block with T-Black. He was also there when the shootout with the cops went down. T-Black took the beef, so Four-Five made sure he wanted for nothing up state, commissary, sneakers, TVs, radios, tablets and anything else money could afford the hommie. He also made sure his mom Karen Black was taken care of too. Four-Five standing six foot two, in shape, light skinned nigga with light green eyes, three sixty waves, trimmed full beard.

Only twenty nine years old, wanting to shift his dirty money into legal business by the age thirty, so he can leave the game and its stresses behind. Besides he's evaded jail for a long time, each day now he's throwing rocks at the pen. His endgame doesn't consist of looking over his shoulder every day, ending up like Big Butch. "That nigga liked being flashy and the center of attention". Four-Five said then added. "When you move with car loads, it's easier to spot you. That's why I move like I do". Four-Five only trusted T-Black, knowing he would hold him down til his last breath. Four-Five's cell phone sounding off. He looked down seeing it's one of his players ready to grab two bricks. It was coded in how many times the phone rang before they hung up, followed by texting the location. " Yo let's hit Chan's up for some chicken wings and fried rice". Four-Five said standing up from the couch. "I have to bless them folks with two of them". He added, securing his twin nickel plated .45 Desert Eagles on his back side under his white T-shirt. They exited the crib together looking around as they got into the midnight blue 760Li BMW with the AMG package, chrome flakes in the custom paint, plush black leather interior, JBL system, TVs throughout, nine inch TV in the dashboard doubling as the navigational system. Dark tinted windows allowing them to conceal the occupants and whatever business is conducted inside. It didn't take long before they made it uptown to 6th and Mclay Streets where the Chinese take out is located in the Edmont Plaza. When they exited the whip each of them scanning the area seeing cars parked music blasting as niggas leaning up against their whips eating the Chinese take out. T-Black concealing his Tek-9 under his light Sean Jean spring jacket. When they entered the take out spot, they seen two females at the counter with this nigga off to the side of them awaiting them to place they order.

"I want two shrimp egg rolls, some pork fried rice and chicken wings. She wants pork rib tips and French fries. Oh give me a order of General Tso too". The female said sounding off her order. The Asian man behind the counter turning to the others in the back speaking Cantonese, calling out the order just placed. Along with making the boss aware that he has company awaiting him. " How can I help you sir?" The Asian man asked coming from the back over to Four-Five. "I asked for chicken wings and rice. They gave me rib tips and sweet and sour". Four-Five responded, handing the bag with the two kilos in it over to the Asian man. "One minute, I'll fix that for you". He said turning speaking his native tongue vanishing to the back, before returning minutes later. "Here you go sir, sorry for the inconvenience". He said. The Asian man is Joel Li, a forty year old, standing five foot seven, slim built, clean shaven, black hair combed back. A quiet hustler supplying the Asian community, his white clientele seeking the raw powder fish scale, along with those who visit his family's nightclub Tao, located on Cameron Street. Four-Five and T-Black exited making their way into the car, opening the bag, seeing the ten grand blocks of money counted out. T-Black put the whip in reverse when another car was passing by unaware of their surroundings. He blew the horn getting their attention. " Stupid ass shit, niggas don't be paying attention". T-Black said driving off, turning the music up blasting Unda Armor, By Jamaican artist Beam. Close to four blocks later they're being followed by TK and his ride or die bitches Suga Baby and Tati. "Let me get one of them chicken wings Tati?" TK said sitting in the passenger seat."Pull up on this nigga so I can get his attention". TK added, eating the chicken wing. He rolled the window down as they came to the stop light at 6th and Reilly Streets. He tossed the chicken wing out the window on to the front windshield of 760Li BMW.

"I know this bitch ass nigga didn't throw this shit on purpose disrespecting my whip?" T-Black snapped, reaching for his Tek-9 aiming it towards the Panamera Porsche, ready to check this nigga until the Panamera pulled off when the light turned green. T-Black mashing the gas following behind the Porsche feeling some type a way about this disrespect. Four-Five on the other hand, not thinking it was disrespect, more like a accident. "Fuck them dick heads, we have to focus on this paper. We can't snap every time shit gets out of line. It only side tracks us from this paper". Four-Five said. T-Black listening pulling over to remove the partially eaten wing from his windshield since it wedged in. At the same time, he noticed the Porsche Panamera reverse lights come on, as the car raced towards him. He didn't hesitate to make his Tek-9 visible. The Porsche is still coming. Then it happened. Tati popping out of the sun roof with a Mac-11 spraying T-Black thrusting his body back, lifting him up only to slam down hard on the ground. The Panamera came to a halt. At the same time Four-Five started squeezing the triggers on both of his .45 Desert Eagles sending slugs through the windshield into Tati's face and body slumping her as the brute force of the slugs sucked the life from her flesh. Suga Baby slamming the gear into park jumping out with a Glock 40mm, along with TK rushing over with his twin 9mm Berettas unleashing a barrage of bullets into the car finding Four-Five over and over, face body, legs leaving him with no escape, other than death. "Let's get the fuck out of here!" TK yelled seeing Four-Five slumped over. They jumped in the car she mashed the gas racing off going zero to a hundred in under six seconds. TK pulling Tati's lifeless body into the car. Suga Baby taking a look, broke down. "They killed my bitch! I can't believe this shit! We should have killed that nigga in Chan's". She vented. TK having the drop on Four-Five knowing Joel Li, was moving work, so he got him to lure Four-Five uptown to take him out. He didn't want to make the Chinese take out spot hot, handling business there, so he waited. It worked out, even if he didn't get a chance to take Four-Five's money and drugs, only his position of power, which is the more important factor right now. TK is a step closer to what he has envisioned for so long up state stuck in the cell hearing about how these cats was eating out here. "Calm down and stay focus. We can't bring her back. What we can do is hold her legacy down, by taking this shit over". He said before pausing to wipe Suga Baby's tears away. " We got this shit. I ain't going to let nothing happen to you. I put my life on it, you hear me?" He said now knowing her and Tati is some real thugged out ass bitches. Too bad Tati caught slugs, because she could have witness the rise of this take over he has set his mind on for many years, awaiting to come home and put it all in play, like now. "Yeah, I hear you". She said driving in and out of the streets, making their escape, before driving into a alleyway, dropping Tati's body off, to be discovered in the hood, but first Suga Baby had a brief moment with her girl, kissing her still warm lips goodbye one last time. "I see you on the other side bitch". Suga baby said before leaving, ditching and burning the Panamera Porsche, ridding it of any evidence that would trace back to them. TK nor Suga Baby knew T-Black was wearing a bullet proof vest. Each slug Tati fired halted by the vest, however the brute force of the slugs bruised his chest, knocking him unconscious until medics and police officers arrived, awaking him with smelling salt, only to question and arrest him for possession of a unlawful fire arm having the Tek-9. He later bailed out with one focus in mind. To avenge his hommie by tracking down these mutha fuckas that killed him, making them pay in blood...

Chapter 3

Harrisburg Police Station. Homicide Detectives Tim Ritter and his partner Donnie Wilson are going over the video footage of the surrounding area where the shootout occurred between Four-Five, T-Black, TK and his ride or die bitches. All happening in close proximity of the federal building, the twenty four hour mini mart and the Bethesda Mission. Multiple angles in high definition. TK having a baseball cap on, with shades, his head at the perfect angle, not that he planned it. It went in his favour, with them not being able to identify him. As for Suga Baby and Tati, their pretty faces and deadly behavior all caught on camera, along with her custom painted Porsche Panamera they escaped in. The feed showing how the cars turning the corner, followed by the BMW stopping, then the female popping out of the sunroof opening fire. "No regard for life or respect for the law, having the federal building right there". Detective Ritter said. Tim Ritter, a white male standing five foot ten, thick build, full pronounced mustache, the rest of his face clean. Piercing blue eyes, brown hair and a deep voice. A dedicated detective, that's persistent in all the cases he takes on. "Now look at these two, jumping out like this is the wild west. I bet the girl on top didn't make it the way the slugs jolted her body. We now have to find her body, hoping it will point to the other two". Detective Wilson said. The Afro-American standing six foot even, bald head, full beard with Beijing black dye in it, covering the grey hairs. Only forty seven, the stress of the job, brought on the grey hairs. "We don't even have to wait that long, pause the video". Detective Ritter said, pointing at the license plate, then added. " We run the plate, then we hit the house it's registered to". "I'm a screen shot the images, send them to my CIs to see what they know about these three". Detective Wilson said taking images of TK and Suga Baby firing on Four-Five through the windshield.

Both now wanted for homicide and attempted homicide for shooting T-Black. While the detectives rounded up officers to head out to Suga Baby's house on the Hill Side of the city, on North Street in the fifteen hundred block, T-Black was at his crib in the SmithHolmes projects on Cameron Street, securing weapons; 9mm Uzi with a hundred round clip. A nickel plated 40mm, he tucked on his waist line. He didn't like that this bitch shot him, plus killed his hommie. Now he plans to track them down for that stupid shit. Unlike the methods the cops are using to track the tags, he's going to hit the

The Crown Is Mine

streets, putting money up to flush them out. It shouldn't be hard with the visual image of the custom painted Panamera Porsche still in his head. Somebody in the hood has to know who this bitch is. He would start with her then find out who the rest is. T-Black exited the crib making his way to his GS450 Lexus all black, even the 24 inch rims, with the black interior making the light tint even look dark. He opened the door to his whip when he spotted two young hustlas trapping. "Aye yo!" He called out waiving them over. "What's good OG?" The little hustlas asked still gripping the money from the fiend they just served. "Y'all niggas be seeing that candy apple red, Porsche Panamera come through here?" T-Black asked making them think she was looking for him. "Nah but shorty that be pushing that whip is nice with a fat ass". The young buck said dapping his hommie, who agreed. "Hold up, that's yo chick OG?" The other young hustla asked. "Nah I was just trying to get at her so I can put it down on that fat ass booty". He responded making the young niggas laugh. " She be moving around on the Hill a lot". The young buck said. "What about that pretty bitch she be with?" "I see them riding all the time so if you bag one, let the other one know we trying to get at her, young niggas doing grown up shit". The young buck responded cuffing his nuts, thinking about Suga Baby.

T-Black jumped in his whip, driving off with his gun now on his lap ready to rock out if he came face to face with the mutha fuckas that hit him up. He want them not only to bleed, they too will feel the brute force and pain of multiple slugs slamming into their flesh. Tough as he is, even with the vest, that shit hurt like a mutha fucka. Now with Four-Five gone, T-Black would also have to step up in his place, holding the hood down, while looking after Four-Five's mom and two kids that depended on him for everything. The thought of this angered him, knowing he would have to come over to Four-Five's mom's crib without him being present, looking into his kid's face wishing he could have saved his hommie from this ambush. T-Black drove around to different hoods he fuck with in this getting money game, checking to see if niggas or bitches knew about the pretty thug chick that shot at him and his hommie. He was tuned in smoking blunts of wet, ready to put that work in on sight. The niggas in the hood, seeing how wetted up and pissed off he is, they didn't want no problems, so they directed him as much as they could away from their hood, so they can get this paper, without this crazy nigga shooting shit up. T-Black continued driving around getting closer with information, now having the name of the owner of he Porsche Panamera; Suga Baby. A name she got having ballas and older men she met on line spend they're money on her just to be in her presence, some never even getting a kiss with the way she teased them, yet they still gave her money with hopes of fucking her sexy ass, as they imag-

The Crown Is Mine

ine. T-Black didn't care about none of that shit, when he looked her up in Instagram seeing what she looks like and what she is into. For him, she is as good as dead when he sets eyes on her, putting bullets in her pretty ass face...

Chapter 4

The police now having Kiesha 'Suga Baby' Jackson's house on North Street surrounded, closing in on the front and back door. Both Homicide Detectives Ritter and Wilson with their guns out, standing off to the side of the door. Wilson covering the eye of the door camera to prevent them from seeing the cops. They knocked on the door followed by ringing the doorbell. "Who is it?" A young male voice came over the intercom of the doorbell. "Harrisburg Police, we have a warrant for Keisha Jackson". " She ain't here". The seventeen year old baby brother of Suga Baby said, trying to focus on playing PS5 Ghost Recon. He didn't like the fact the cops is side tracking him from his mission inside of the game. "We need a adult to come to the door to verify this, or we will kick the door in". Detective Ritter said. A silence fell as Jermaine continued playing his game ignoring the cops. The doorbell sounding off again. " I told you she ain't here, now leave me the fuck alone, y'all messing me up". Jermaine snapped taking on fire in the game. At the same time a loud booming sound of the front door being breached could be heard throughout the house. The sound jolting the young teen. He removed his head set, taking hold of his cell phone calling his sister. "What's up baby bro?" Suga Baby asked. "The cops just kicked in the door coming in the house". He responded nervously. " Let me see your hands!" Detective Wilson yelled out rushing up the steps, seeing the teen standing at the top. Jermaine froze in fear of being gunned down, or his phone being mistaken for a gun. "Let me see your other hand!" Detective Wilson said, noticing Jermaine's right hand was out of sight. He quickly raised his right hand fearing he would be shot. "Who else is in the house?" Detective Wilson asked coming up on the kid. "Nobody, my mom went to the corner store". " Where's your sister?" "What?" He responded stalling out, knowing his sister is on the phone listening in, before hanging up.

Suga Baby and TK was close by, hoping to secure some things before moving on to his spot on the edge of the city. A quiet area his grandmother left him when she passed away while he was in jail. His grand mom favouring him for all he's done for her when he was home even when he first went to jail he gave her money to comfort her. "I told y'all my sister not here. My mom is going to be pissed y'all kicked her door in". Jermaine said watching the uniformed officers move through the house searching. Detective Ritter came up to Jermaine. "Next time we say open the door, you do it instead of playing that stupid ass game that could have gotten you shot with real bullets". Detective Ritter said pointing his gun in Jermaine's face, taunting him. Jermaine cutting his eye at the detective, angered by his approach. "Tell your sister, and her friends they can run, we will track them down". Detective Wilson said before making his way down the steps. As he's heading down his phone sounded off, he picked up on the second ring. " Detective Wilson here". "Wilson this is Officer Logan, we have a female victim fitting your description, same clothes and bullet wounds to match the picture from the car you sent us". " Where at?" "Third ward". " I'm not far from there I'm on my way". He said ending the call, looking back up the steps at his partner having a one on one with Jermaine. "Ritter we have our second suspect DOA in the third ward". Detective Wilson said. Ritter started down the steps not realizing Jermaine was giving both of them the finger, before hurrying to text his sister. Jermaine: They leaving, saying they found 2nd Vic DOA. Suga Baby: Sorry baby bro. Tell ma I luv her, I'll Bfine. Jermaine: Luv U2 sis, Bsafe. As Jermaine pulled himself together the detectives were driving to the third ward, pulling up on the narrow alleyway like street seeing taped off area. They pulled over exiting the car ducking under the yellow crime scene tape, immediately seeing the lifeless body of Tatiana. Her face marred from the slugs that took a chunk of her face and skull. "Yeah that's definitely our suspect. I told you the slugs she caught put her down". Detective Wilson said looking on at the holes in her mid section made by the . 45 Desert Eagles, along with her eye socket blown out from the powerful slug that entered her eye, ripping a chunk of the back of her head off. "Did you find any ID Officer Logan?" Detective Ritter asked. "I didn't touch anything. I secured the area, then made the call". "Okay, I guess we'll do the honors". Detective Ritter said taking out a pair of black latex gloves putting them on. He searched her pockets removing two magnum condoms. "Well we at least know what she prefers. Too bad she won't be needing these anymore". Detective Ritter said trying to have a sense of humor in this serious situation, giving a brief smirk. "Your mind is fucked up partner, now find something we can use to further this case ". He did just that removing credit cards along with her driver's license. All saying her name is Tatiana Winters. "Officer Logan, await the coroner to pick her up, here's her things. We already know who she is now, and how she died. This case for her is closed. Now we have to track down the other two". T-Black is amongst the crowd of people looking on, seeing the bitch that shot him is dead, meaning the hommie Four-Five didn't go out without putting in work, making someone pay in blood. T-Black was slipping off also trying to figure who the other two are, so he can get them before the cops do. The detectives got into their unmarked Chevy Impala driving off when they spotted T-Black. They pulled up on him, Detective Wilson rolling down the passenger window. "I don't believe in coincidences. You got booked for the gun and the bullet proof vest beef. The girl over there, we assume tried to take you out, so now you want to pop back at anyone riding with her? I'm a tell you this, let that shit go.

Chapter 5

It's our job to handle those involved in this case". Detective Wilson said staring at T-Black seeing the dark murderous look in his eyes, knowing he wants revenge by any means. They can't just lock him up, to assure he doesn't seek blood and revenge. They can only advise him not to make their job harder with him wishing to do ill will, wanting to honor the code of the streets with a bloody payback. Wilson also having ran a background check on T-Black seeing he will put work in on anyone in his way, especially having been in a shoot out with cops when he was a teen. T-Black not even phased by Detective Wilson's attempt to deter him from what he has his heart and mind set on. They disrespected his gangsta, which means they have to face what's coming to them. "We all have a job to do out here. I plan on keeping you two employed. Them bitches came at me like it's a game, I'm a show them who really winning out here". He stated firmly fueled by his anger, as he flashed back to the slugs slamming I to his chest. "This ain't no mutha fucking game!" Detective Ritter snapped, "Real people, real lives and families are being effected by all of these stupid ass decisions y'all making!" T-Black turned ignoring the detective, blending into the crowd of bystanders disappearing to his whip, set on finding these two that disrespected his gangsta. "I can't believe this idiot wanting to take this shit into his own hands. I know he's pissed about getting shot, shit I would be mad, but he can't run the city like that". Detective Ritter added, driving off hoping to find his two homicide suspects before T-Black does leaving a bloody massacre... anyone, or allowing anybody to get close to him. He turned his head looking up at her. She leaned in placing a kiss to this forehead. "I can wait, I'm not going anywhere. I'm a ride with you until my last breath". She said effortlessly, like they've known one another for years. His demeanor is what she became accustom to over the last two weeks. It brought her closer to him, having respect for him being a caretaker, a man of his word. Over the last two weeks he went out shopping, getting them food, clothing, and feminine items for her catering to her needs, with her being unable to leave the house with cops looking for her. " Who we hitting up next?" She asked. "Some Spanish chick I heard about up state. They call her La Reina, that shit means The Queen". TK said. Suga Baby smiling having heard of her, knowing she lives in the condo high rise uptown overlooking the city and Susquehanna River. A five thousand square foot condo with all of the amenities one can afford

The Crown Is Mine

giving her comfort. " You know this bitch?" TK asked. "Not personally, only seeing her around at the malls, clubs, restaurants and the city. She always move with a team, even in her pink Lamborghini, they right behind her in the Range Rovers". "What about the stories of her being a cartel princess and a shooter, is it true?" He questioned, wanting to know what he's up against. "She's not only a killer, she's a bad bitch these hoes out here be trying to be like. She knows somebody from Mexico or South America. The Queen is the female affiliation of Latin Kings". Suga Baby said. Hearing this made it all too real for him, knowing if he took her down robbing or killing her, he can never be pegged as the one that did it. La Reina's connect along with Latin Kings would get at him. This Queen chick is a boss in a position TK wants, and she's in the way, so he has to think this through to make it all play out to his advantage. So he can sit at the top literally and figuratively speaking.

"You still with me, even knowing who this Spanish chick is?" He asked her, since she knows a lot about Tiara 'La Reina' Rodrigez, a five foot nine boss latina with sparkling grey eyes, flowing with her silky long black hair caressing her shoulders down to her ass. A radiant smile with perfect white teeth she paid for, 34C breast, small waist, a curvy booty, long legs adding to the visual. A tattoo of a crown on her neck worn by a lioness roaring. The initials LQ in the crown, standing for Latin Queen.

Tiara is only twenty eight years old, looking like a youthful twenty year old, captivating soft appeal, never to be mistaken or misjudged. In doing so, one would meet their demise after humiliation and torture. The streets of Harrisburg loved her for all she did for the Spanish community, the youth giving back, helping single mothers and struggling fathers that raised children in the hard streets of the city. Her reach is also throughout the state getting respect in every hood the Latin Kings are, for her beauty and deadly approach. "She's a bad bitch, but I'm not to be fucked with". Suga Baby responded, knowing she has nothing other than her life to lose. " Now let's figure out how we going to take her down". Suga Baby added sitting at his side. He was looking on at her, appreciating her real gangsta side. She's tougher than most of these fake ass niggas out here in the streets. "Once we handle this, I'm a get a lay low spot out of the way, so you can chill securing the money while I take this shit over". He said, wanting to protect her from jail. "It's take over season, and I want to be at your side until we get to the top. I'm not a back seat type bitch, to watch it all go down". Suga Baby said grabbing hold of the gun off the table loading it, her mindset shifting to beast mode, ready take what she wants. He gave a brief laughter and smile tripping off her gangsta side that is coming all of the way out, letting a nigga no Suga Baby ain't that sweet.

Chapter 6

The sun is setting on the city, as TK made his move walking into the condo building passing the front desk, already having the address, thanks to Suga Baby's early reconnaissance, when she entered close to thirty minutes ago. TK wearing shades, a Dominos pizza baseball cap and shirt, totting a pizza bag with two large pizzas inside, along with his Tek-22. He paid a delivery kid two hundred dollars for the gear and pizza. He was excited about the tip so he gave it to him. TK got into the elevator pressing the top floor button, thinking about every scenario as the elevator ascended. Each thought graphic, yet in his favor. He was ready for whatever having the Tek-22 inside the pizza bag, along with two glock 40s on his back tucked in his pants. The elevator doors opened, he turned towards the condo, seeing two Spanish goons looking like NFL line men. They also spotted TK walking toward them with the pizza bag in hand. The closer he got to them, the more alert they became, knowing anyone or anything coming to this condo, they would be fully aware of it. The big Latino on the right is reaching into his suit jacket, while the other is holding his hand up to slow or stop TK. "Que pasa amigos, I got pizza for the queen". TK said, now a few yards away. Right then, they both removed their .45 automatic weapons aiming at TK. " No body at this address eats pizza". The big Latino said firmly staring at TK. La Reina disliked pizza since her childhood. All her goons and close associates knew this. They didn't know this, but was prepared for multiple scenarios to this take down. Suga Baby turned the corner making her presence known, having been tuned in via airpod ear piece listening in. "That's my pizza, why y'all keep delivering it to the wrong place". She said strutting her beauty in three inch pumps, white YSL jeans hugging her curves, flowing up to her powder blue top, that's caressing her nipples tweaking them, giving a visual show to anyone standing in front of her. The white and gold Gucci hand bag she's approaching with is hiding twin .380s with pearl handles, along with extra clips. The two goons now placing their weapons back in their suits, seeing Suga Baby coming to claim the pizza. She stuck her hand into the bag as she closed in. "How much is it?" Now a few feet away. TK opening the pizza bag reaching for the Tek-22, responding to her. "This is going to be some expensive pizza". She smiled removing the twin .380s aiming one at each of the goons. "You can make it home to your families, or your family can go to the funeral home to see what good job they did in covering

40

The Crown Is Mine

up the bullet holes in your face". Suga Baby said looking sexy and deadly all at once. TK stripped them of their weapons placing one on his waist line, the other tucking it on the small of Suga Baby's back side, in them tight white jeans. "You know what it is. We need inside the condo. Anything go wrong I'll leave you right here". TK said firmly pressing his gun to the big goons back. The Latino body guard using his key card and code, a dual security feature opening the door. Soon as they entered, everything sped up with gunfire erupting from the two body guards that stood fifteen feet on the other side of the door. The slugs slamming into the other two Latinos as TK and Suga Baby hid behind them, using their large flesh as shields, only to return a barrage of bullets crashing into the faces and bodies of the two goons. TK and Suga Baby rushing into the condo, knowing they don't have much time to secure what they came for; Money and or the location to where the cocaine is. Soon as the entered the open living space, they can see La Reina standing over by the floor to ceiling window with a double shot of Patron in her glass enjoying the sunset and the city skyline. Now less than ten feet away from her, Suga Baby aiming at her from the front, TK having his gun pointed from the side. La Reina still calm, not phased by their abrupt presence.

"Death is the only thing truly promised when you stick around this business long enough". Tiara said staring out the window enjoying the view. " This is why insurance is important. My interior, exterior security systems and cameras have your images. You can kill me, then my people will kill your entire family, then and only when they're all dead and gone, they'll torture and kill you both. So is this power you seek, worth the pain and wrath that will be imposed?" Tiara asked. "We don't have to kill her". Suga Baby said, knowing they just came for the money or product. "Shut the fuck up! We came this far. It's about money, the power, and I'm hungry for both". TK snapped. Tiara still calm looking at TK now. "Power huh? Saying it feels good until it's your reality. You want money, there's close to two million in my walk in closet". "That's chump change to you. I want the product too". TK said. She laughed before drinking the double shot of Patron. "And then what? You think with my money and product you'll be able to move the cocaina in this city or state as long as I'm breathing. Dead or alive, this doesn't end well for you or anyone you love". Tiara said holding on to her position of power. Suga Baby in fear of the all too real threats, squeezed off rounds on Tiara, dropping her where she stood, wounding her. "I guess we all in now". TK said looking at Suga Baby. "You heard what she said. We leave her alive, we're a target. I thought you wanted me to ride with you?" She said standing her ground with the decision to shoot La Reina. TK made his way over to the downed queen bitch pointing his gun

42

The Crown Is Mine

at her face seeing the blood coming from her mouth, due to organs being hit. "I'm a take my chances with this next level of power, with my ride or die right there". "Fuck you puta!" Tiara said. TK fired a single shot into her pretty face before running to the bedroom securing the money with Suga Baby. They took the money that was closer to three million.

They fled the condo using the fire escape down to the parking garage where the stolen Nissan Maxima is. They hopped in driving off fast and far from this crime scene that is allowing them to feel the power of this take over. "What's next for us? We can't stay here now, it's not smart or safe". Suga Baby said. "We bounce until shit gets back right for the take over. We have enough to adjust anywhere we go, even down south, plus we got them bricks, we can bubble with down there, then come back to PA strong". "What about that shit with the insurance she was talking about?" Suga Baby asked thinking about her mom and baby brother. "We good, she was trying to flex her position and power on us". He responded down playing Tiara's words and long reach in this game, being a connected gang member. Not realizing every word spoken was the truth. "Now off that subject, I'm hungry as a mutha fucka. What you want to eat before we get our shit and bounce?" TK added feeling the rush of murder and taking what he pleases. Suga Baby looking on at him also getting a rush, turned on by him even more now.

"I'm hungry for you". She said placing her hand on his thigh, sliding up his leg. He got hard immediately, having her soft hand on him. He put his hand on hers. "We have plenty of money and time to do this the right way, for the first time. I want it to be slow, hard, deep, intimate and memorable". He said. "Damn, you make it sound so good, I can't wait. You better not have a little dick either". She said laughing hard, also making him laugh too, at how wild and outspoken she is. A side most would never get to see. "I would whip it out for you to take a visual measurement, but I don't think you would be satisfied with just looking, you would want it right here and now. I'm not trying to crash or get caught". He responded driving to get rid of the stolen car, to another rental he had on stand by...

The Crown Is Mine

Chapter 7

While TK and Suga Baby was on 695 passing the Capitol BeltWay, heading down south. The Homicide detectives are all over the fresh crime scene at the condo belonging to Tiara 'La Reina' Rodrigez, a sanctioned gang member with the Latin Kings, also backed by Cartel Lieutenant Eguardo 'Budda' Sanchez who handles business out of Reading, PA, controlling distribution from Chicago to the tristate area. The detectives aware of her gang association, not the cartel connection. "This could be a gang hit, from the looks of things, taking out her four bodyguards, then her. A inside job even since she doesn't allow people to get close to her". Detective Ritter said. "I doubt that detective, the building security said he seen a male and female leaving in a hurry carrying bags, one wearing Dominos uniform". Officer Roman said. "I want footage from entry to exit of those you speak of". Detective Wilson said, then turned to his partner. "You think it's the same two that did the shooting two weeks ago?" "Either that or it's a new trending thing with a Bonnie and Clyde theme". A voice with a strong Spanish accent came from behind the detectives. "Whoever is responsible, I feel sorry for them and everyone they love". The detectives turning around seeing this six foot even Latino, clean shaven, well groomed, black hair combed back, black color eyes, dressed GQ wearing a two piece Armani cream color suit, flowing with the tan leather Armani loafers, leather band on his AP watch, no diamonds needed for this look of power, along with the imported hand rolled Cuban cigar. "Who the hell is this guy on my crime scene?" Detective Ritter asked looking around. No one said anything. "I'm a family friend as well as a deep cover federal Agent Sanchez". Making his identity somewhat known to them. He is the Cartel Lieutenant Eguardo 'Budda' Sanchez. A stone cold killer since a young kid living in Sinaloa, Mexico. His uncle Hector Sanchez encouraged him to get his citizenship, that later allowed him to become a federal agent, staying connected to all Intel against the family, while assisting with distribution, in multiple states. Being a agent, this gave him power and free reign over the cocaine distribution. Budda stopped by today as planned for a intimate evening with his number one product mover and sexy ass bitch, La Reina. She also owed him a couple million, which is another reason she had more in her closet than she stated. "Agent Sanchez we appreciate your presence, this is a homicide crime scene". Detective Wilson said. "Yes it is, and if you don't want multiple crime scenes, you need to get all of the camera footage inside and out of this condo to track down whoever is responsible. Otherwise mi amigo, this city will be turned upside down, having her gang family terrorizing all to find answers and justice themselves". Budda said leaving them with that thought, as he walk into La Reina's bedroom over to the walk in closet. A few stacks of money left behind, not even a hundred grand remaining. TK and Suga Baby came up big time. All of her diamonds and watches untouched. The jewelry collection worth over million. This alone let him know, whoever did this wasn't a petty criminal the way they came for her. Now he'll use his resources in the agency, securing the footage from this building to find out himself who was involved. More important who they're related to, so they can pay with their lives, until he can get his money and revenge for a woman he was intimately into and falling for. A relationship that should have never taken place, with the level of business being conducted between the two of them. Her beauty luring him into her personal space outside of cocaine distribution. Budda took hold of a picture of Tiara off the night stand, wearing a red bikini on a white sand beach, looking like a model smiling at the camera. "I'll take care of this mi amor". He kissed the photo, flashing to memories, pained by it all.

Budda staring at the picture gritting his teeth, thinking about getting revenge for her death. He took the picture out of the frame kissing it, since this is the closest he'll get to her warm lips, now that she's gone forever. He placed the picture inside his jacket pocket, for memories. He exited the room coming back out to the gangland style massacre, seeing the marred face of this once rare beauty he shared intimate nights with. He placed his hand over his heart, also where the picture of her is. "They will pay for this mi amor". He said in a low tone, as he looked around the condo observing point of entry, along with camera angles inside the condo. The downed goons that was her security. They too took on a barrage of bullets, he noticed. He's now having thoughts of securing the video footage himself instead of waiting on the homicide detectives to get it. "Whoever it was came for money. Traces of that can be found in the bedroom, leaving the rest of the money behind". Budda said. "What the hell was this guy doing in the bedroom?" Detective Wilson asked still wondering what real interest the FBI has in this homicide case. It's something about his presence that is not sitting right with either detective, especially with him being a lone federal agent with concern of this case. "Are you done roaming around on our crime scene?" Detective Ritter asked. "I hope you two solve this case with that same energy you have focused on me. Other wise this city will be in a lot of trouble chasing a trail of bodies that will be left behind in the wake of her demise". Budda said turning to exit, leaving them to do things their way, while he's going to take matters in his own hands, with a cartel approach, no mercy or regrets for those responsible or connected to the ones who killed his love interest and financial investment, La Reina, a powerful gang member with deep rooted ties to people who respect and have loyalty to her...

Chapter 8

After twelve hours of nonstop driving, TK and Suga Baby arrived in Atlanta, Georgia. They checked in at a Days Inn where they took showers before falling asleep next to one another, being exhausted, the intimate side of things weren't even on their minds five in the morning. The adrenaline from taking out La Reina and her goons, wore off. The continuous thoughts of what's next also wore on their minds and bodies making them completely tired. 12:08PM TK was jolted from his sleep hearing the sounds of police radios outside of his room. His eyes wide open, he jumped out of the bed securing one of the glock 40s, rushing over to the window peeping through the curtain. He sighed seeing it's a couple next door having a domestic dispute that brought the attention of the cops. This abrupt dose of adrenaline surging through his body is better than coffee. He's wide awake now. He turned away from the window walking back to the bed seeing the sleeping Suga Baby resting peacefully, looking sexy in her short pajamas shorts by Victoria Secret, showing off her smooth legs, thick thighs, and fat ass as she's laying on her stomach, facing him. He sat the gun down, coming over climbing on the bed, placing kisses to her inner thighs up to her butt. His kisses trailing up to her side, her eyes opening to this pleasurable feeling of affectionate kisses. "Mmh, I like to be awaken with intimate kisses". She said turning over looking in his eyes wanting him. He leaned in kissing her lips, then her neck, she welcomed this feeling. His kisses going back to where they started, sliding her pink pajamas shorts off gracefully, exposing her waxed art of paradise and passion. He leaned in coming close to her pulsating flesh and protruding clitoris. He placed a soft kiss, followed by his tongue extending to touch her clit. She let out a heated breath. " Don't tease me". She said waiting for this intimate moment. He too have waited for ten years, fantasizing about all the freaky shit he wants to do with females when he gets home, now he's face to face with this sweet smelling pussy he's ready to take his time eating and treating it to the D. He introduced his left index finger into her body that's wet, heated, yearning his touch. His tongue followed caressing her clitoral pearl, creating a sensation she fell weak to. Her heart is fluttering the faster his finger and tongue is moving, stirring a powerful surge of butterflies in her belly, bouncing around, just as she is squirming across the bed moaning. "Oooh, Oooh, Oooh God, Oooh, damn this is good. Oooh, oooh your tongue is good to my body, Oooh, oooh, Oooh God". Her moans intensifying as orgasmic wave is racing through her body, ready to escape. " Oooh no, Oooh my God, Mmmh, Mmmh". She moaned unable to slide any more with her body being backed to the head board, now she's trapped to embrace the intense pleasure and play of his tongue and finger. She can't hold back the surging sensation, that's rushing through her body. Her legs is tightening, stomach clenching full of that butterfly like sensation, her moans heated. One hand on his head the other grabbing a fist full of sheets, her eyes are closed mouth open allowing this orgasmic pleasure and pressure to be released. The flow from her body over his tongue and finger. He can feel it with her being a squirter. When it came to a slow, it made her body super sensitive. He halted the intimate foreplay, looking at her now biting lightly on her lip. "You ready for the best part?" He said fully exposed to her. She smiled seeing his pulsating nine and a half inch dick with a thick head. "I'm ready". She responded excited to finally have him. She extended her soft hand taking hold of his length and thickness, guiding it in. She let out a moan feeling his manhood creating pleasure filled pressure on her body. "Aaah, aaah, aaah". She moaned as he pressed into her deep, hitting her bottom. Her legs wrapping around him as he took, long deep strokes, side to side, in and out. Their minds, hearts and bodies into this, making each stroke intense and intimate. "Aah, aaah, aaah, this is good dick, aaah, aaah, aaah,

aaah,". He started going faster and harder. Her moans and orgasmic sensation surging through her body with each powerful stroke thrusting deep inside of her. She thought he was about to bust, with his speed picking up, until he stopped turning her over, doggy style. Her head down as his thumb is pressing on her asshole creating intense pleasure, matched by the throbbing thickness of his dick slamming into her faster and harder. " Ooooh God, aaah, aaah, ooooh my God, aaah, aaah, I'm cuming, mmmh, mmmh," She moaned as the wave surged through her body. His fast deep strokes also because he too is now ready to erupt, having waited so long for this right here. He can't hold back, his strokes reaching deep as his body let go of the powerful eruption spraying into her warm wet body. Her vaginal muscles contracting on him as she's having orgasms, making each of their experience even more intense and sensational. He paused allowing it to take its natural course before removing himself from her. She turned around, taking hold of him licking her juices off the thick head, before placing her soft lips on him, stroking with her soft hands, making him come alive erecting to full attention. Her smooth lips gliding over him, making him close his eyes, falling weak to her oral magic. "You a beast". He let out feeling himself busting again in her mouth. She swallowed, still stroking to get it all. She made a popping sound when her lips came off his dick. She started laughing. "Now this was all worth the wait. I wish my bitch Tati was here to get some of this". "I told you I got you. Now that we have that out of the way, we focus on the take over, and we can fuck like this whenever you want or think about it". TK said. "I look forward to more of this. Cause I'm a ride with you all the way ".

She said looking on at him with loving eyes, not realizing he put it down on her with the tongue and dick, having her open from the orgasms. He picked up on the look too. "I got you baby girl. Ain't nothing going to happen to you as long as I'm around". He said leaning in kissing her forehead affectionately. She can feel the emotion of love in her body. Maybe it's the powerful orgasms she had coupled with the fact they're both in a vulnerable state of fleeing and in need of someone they can trust with their all, including intimafcy. "Keisha Jackson, that's my real name. I wanted you to know the real me. I am what you see and will be the wildest bitch you'll ever meet". She said professing commitment to him. "Yeah that's why I fuck with you Suga Baby, you don't have a filter of lies only the truth. TK is my initials. Tracy King is my name, which means in the streets the crown is mine, because my mutha fucking last name says so, which makes you my queen, you sexy beast". He stated. She pulled him close for a passionate kiss that lead to another round of heated explosive sex...

Chapter 9

Back up north in Harrisburg, Pennsylvania Federal Agent and Cartel Lieutenant Eguardo 'Budda' Sanchez, used his federal resources to seize all of the camera footage from the condo Tiara lived in. This means, only he would know who is responsible, therefore they, the detectives wouldn't be in his way of making those responsible pay in blood. This sudden seizure pissed the homicide detectives off, also tweaking their curiosity to why the federal government is so intrigued in this homicide case. Budda didn't care, he had his mind set already. Anyone in his way will meet a violent demise. Budda along with four of his Mexican associates made their way to Emanuel Church on 16th and Liberty Streets located on the Hillside of the city. The church is ran by Reverend Tracy King Senior who preaches there while living in the home next door attached to the church, with his wife, Sister Nancy King of thirty two years. She's a Sunday school teacher. TK only having his parents being the only child, he didn't even have kids. The two Range Rovers pulled in front of the church, the men exited all dressed like businessmen. Sister Nancy is sitting on the porch of her house next door enjoying the weather, when she noticed the men exiting the trucks. She waived at them seeing they're preparing to head up the church steps. "The service starts in a few hours. Bless your hearts for wanting to be first to hear God's word". Sister Nancy said sitting in the chair with her Bible open reading the book of Psalm. "This is your church you go to?" Budda asked. "Yes, my husband is Reverend Tracy King Senior". "Forgive my manners, I'm Federal Agent Sanchez, these are my associates. We came to speak with your son, I assume is Tracy Junior?" Sister Nancy's Godly intuition and motherly instinct kicked in. "What did that boy do now? He just got out of prison". She asked. "If I may come in, I can explain this to you ". She looked at the door of the house, then over to the church.

"The church will be fine, so we can have my husband present to hear what this boy done did". She said coming off the porch. Both of TK's parents are in their sixties, looking preserved, being kept by God and His greatness. She would say. They entered the church, immediately seeing the Reverend behind the altar. "Welcome to the Lord's house. Come one come all as you are to be saved, to be one with God, in the name of Jesus Christ". Reverend King said with his bold voice reaching Budda and his associates, who all paused signing; In the name of the father, the son and the holy spirit. "Amen". They proceeded allowing sister Nancy to lead the way. "These men came to speak to our son. I don't know what he got himself into, but that one right there is FBI". Sister Nancy said pointing at Budda as she stood at her husband's side taking his hand. Reverend King sensing something is wrong, especially scanning their faces not looking the part as they lead his wife to believe they're federal agents. Budda wearing a blue two piece Kenneth Cole suite, tailored to his frame. Black Kenneth Cole shoes, a virgin Mary diamond encrusted pendant on his necklace, flowing with his black face Movado having diamonds at the three, six, nine and twelve o'clock. "My son doesn't live with us as you can see we're God fearing folk. We don't consume or involve ourselves with worldly things or worries". Reverend King said knowing these men aren't who they're projecting to be. The presence of evil is amongst them. "Reverend, the Bible talks about sacrifices all of the time. The most notable sacrifice we all know is what Jesus done for us all. Your son has made a decision in his life of sin, that comes with sacrifices, placing you and your lovely wife in harms way. You may not know where he is, but after today, he'll know where you are". Budda said. His goons removing their weapons. "You can kill the flesh, but we have eternal life with the Lord in heaven". Reverend King said, turning around still holding his wife's hand, looking up at the cross with Jesus on it. Then it happened. Budda's goons squeezed off thunderous rounds sending slugs crashing into their heads and bodies slumping them where they stood looking up at the cross becoming the sacrifice of their son's actions. Reverend King and his wife's souls raced to heaven, after the evil amongst them robbed their flesh killing them off. "Maybe this will get that cabron's attention, making him realized he fucked with the wrong one". Budda said feeling some revenge for his fallen amor, La Reina. "Now let's make that bitch's family pay in blood". He added walking out with his goons as if they didn't just commit the greatest sin, in God's house. Suga Baby's family didn't live too far from the church, being on the same side of the city. Even if they did, he would travel a thousand miles to shed their blood to get his point across. At this point, with the burning rage inside of Budda, no one sharing the same blood as TK or Suga Baby would be safe. He's thinking and feeling as he and his goons exited the church never looking back, as if nothing ever happened. This level of darkness, killing in cold blood in God's house, makes him a diabolical being, that would stop at nothing to appease his sensational appetite for blood and revenge. TK nor Suga Baby would have ever thought of leaving their loved ones behind, knowing this would be the outcome. As promised by La Reina when she made it clear to them, the power they seek wouldn't be as they envisioned. La Reina's people will claim the lives coming for of those responsible for her death, along with all they love. TK originally brushing it off, thinking she was bluffing, trying to flex her position of power. He is now in for a painful wakeup call. A new reality of this level of power he's in search for, and the real life sacrifices he's made with these decision to appease himself with the plans of this takeover he's so hungry for.

Chapter 10

Budda and his goons knocked on the front door of Suga Baby's mom's house, followed by ringing the doorbell. "Can I help you?" Ms. Jackson, Suga Baby's mom asked coming over the intercom. "I'm Federal Agent Sanchez, I would like to speak with you and or your daughter Keisha Jackson". "I'll be down in a second. Don't kick my fucking door in like the last cops did". She said making her way down the stairs, over to the door, opening it, seeing this handsome Latino FBI agent staring back at her. "May I come into discuss your daughter and this case?" Budda asked. "Yes, come on in with your fine self". She responded smiling, checking him out from head to toe. Ms. Jackson a thirty nine year old version of her daughter, showing the beautiful fruit didn't fall far from the tree. "I haven't heard from her since the homicide detectives kicked my door in weeks ago looking for her. Hold on". She said walking to the bottom of the steps yelling up to her son. "Jermaine bring your ass down here now. We have some important people here". Jermaine is in his room playing PlayStation online with his friends. Within minutes he came downstairs seeing the well dressed Latinos, all looking serious. Jermaine being a social media and game consumer all day. He's aware of the internet buzz on this boss chick La Reina being executed. Tweets and IG post speculating heavy retaliation for this Latin Queen gang member. At first glance anyone who isn't in the streets wouldn't pick up on the look of this powerful man before them. For Jermaine, he can see this guy and his goons aren't FBI agents or any type of cops. "My sister didn't do it". "Do what?" Budda asked calmly. "She ain't kill La Reina. That's the buzz online, someone took her out". Budda still remaining calm, having overlooked the social media aspect of this. "When was the last time you spoke to your sister?" "She text me; Good morning, miss you baby bro, this morning". "Call her now, so I can speak with her directly".

"No, why would I do that, so you can lure her in to kill her, or lock her up depending on who you really are, because you don't look like the feds". Jermaine said trying to protect his big sister while standing his ground. Budda removed a cigar and butane lighter, twirling the cigar as he puffed to get it lit. He blew a cloud of smoke into Jermaine's face, then took the butane lighter allowing blow torch like flame to get close to Jermaine's face, where he can feel the heat. At the same time, fear shooting through his body. Ms. Jackson seeing this snapped, trying to fend

The Crown Is Mine

him off verbally until Budda's goons removed their weapons aiming at her. "Get your fucking hands off my son, and tell these ass holes to stop pointing them guns at me!" Ms. Jackson snapped not realizing the magnitude of this present moment. "Now call your sister before my men put a bullet in your mother's face". Jermaine nervously dialed the number face timing his sister. Suga Baby came on the screen looking sexy and dolled up, having that good sex glow, like she ready to step out on the city. She noticed the look of fear in her brother's eyes. "What's wrong baby bro?" Before he could answer, Budda snatched the phone allowing her to have a full visual of who he is and how bad they fucked up. "Who the fuck are you? She asked. "Don't worry yourself with that. You and your friend TK killed a very close associate of mine, who was also a financial investment. For that you put a target on all you love, including yourselves". Suga Baby got up walking to the bathroom where TK is. She banged on the door getting his attention. He opened the door seeing she's pointing at the phone. TK's eyebrows angling, wondering why she still have her phone, when he been got rid of his. TK seen the Latino on the screen. "Now that I have each of your attention. You will pay me the six million you stole in exchange for their lives". "Six million? It wasn't no mutha fucking six million. You trippen nigga".

TK snapped. Budda gave a light laugh, puffing his cigar. "That's the interest for being a thief, and killing my good friend". Budda responded, taking the phone showing his associates with guns aimed at her mom and brother. "The choice is yours. One thing for certain, I'm walking out of this house alive whether you say yes or no. It's up to you, if they live too". Caught in a twisted emotional bind, she almost broke down crying, until TK took control. "Where do you want us to bring the money?" "I'll come to you". He responded quickly. TK knew right then he was lying, either way her family will be murdered, just as they would be if they brought him the money. TK didn't want Suga Baby to have to deal with this painful reality, so he figured to ease her mind, she needed to say her goodbyes. "Let her speak to her mom and baby brother". TK said before muting the phone to speak to her. "Tell your mom and brother, you love them and you'll see them later". TK said. Her eyes becoming glassy fearing this is her last goodbye. He took the phone off mute. Jermaine has the phone. "I love you baby bro. I see you and mom soon okay. I love you mom". She said before handing the phone back to TK, walking away trying absorb the pain of the reality she'll never see her mom or baby brother again. "Come down to Woodlawn, Maryland. Angel Falls Road on a cul de sac. I'll be in the house with double the blue doors". TK said, lying giving up a false description, with hopes of buying time to evade this cartel gangster. Budda also knowing he's lying, so he took the phone standing back so he could see the fear in Ms. Jackson's eyes along with Jermaine. "In case you don't know who you're really fucking with". Budda nodding his head. His men gunning down Jermaine and his mother with multiple slugs killing them over and over, Mexican cartel gangland style, even coming up on their downed bodies putting bullets in their faces, then Budda turned the phone on himself. "I'm coming for you"...

Chapter 11

"Baby girl look at me". TK said coming up to the emotionally distraught Suga Baby. He lift her face up locking eyes on her. He can see her pain and rightfully so. He knows that with the cartel goon gunning down her family, they already did that to his parents, he just have to embrace the pain knowing the reality he put himself in, the moment he decided to chase after the power this business brings. " We going to make them pay for this shit. Once we get the power and position, we go after him". He said pulling her close, allowing her to bury her head into his chest, her tears flowing. TK gritting his teeth processing revenge and being the one who comes out on top. She pulled her head back looking up at TK. "I want to be the one to put a bullet in his face when we get him". She said venting only seeing red and revenge for the love of her mother and baby brother. She want to look in Budda's eyes as she pulls the trigger taking his life. The thoughts alone of that moment is selfgratifying to her. "When the time comes, I'll let you have your way. Right now we have to take the battery out of that phone along with the sim card, and toss it. Then we have to get on the move, in case they tracked our location". "Babe, I mean TK, we can't keep running with all of this cocaine and bags of money. No one will look for us in the hood of this city. This is Black Atlanta, they stick together down here". Suga Baby said, not knowing she's running from Homicide Detectives Ritter and Wilson along with cartel goon Budda. TK is only fleeing from Budda since Agent Sanchez seized the condo building footage, he's the only one that knows both of their identities. As for the other shootings, TK has still not been labeled as one of the shooters due to the angles of the cameras, couldn't make out who he is. "We can't just go to the hood and hide. We have to work our way in. Get the respect, trust and loyalty of the hood". "You're a king, and with me riding as your queen, we'll take control by taking over. We have the cocaine and money to back the shit we talk along with the guns and the heart to use them". Suga Baby said channelling her pain and anger. TK is even more down with her, loving her gangsta approach. "We'll hit the hood, see who's holding it down, who's hungry, wanting more out of this game. First thing we need to do is, dump the phone, move location, secure new phones, and go shopping, to look the part, then get a rental". TK said seeing her shifting her pain to have more focus on what's to come, envisioning her endgame. They parted from the comforting embrace, looking on at one another taking in each other visually. Seeing that they are one another's person, without question. Nothing will tear them apart other than death. Even then, they'll die together. The moment came to an end as she turned heading to the bathroom to get ready for the day ahead. At the same time she needed time alone to truly let out the pain she was feeling, knowing she will never see her baby brother or mother again. She cried silently, before pulling it together staring into the mirror with murderous eyes and a heart seeking the revenge of blood, meaning the life of Budda, for what he's stolen from her, the moment he gave the order to kill her family. TK gravitating towards Suga Baby, wanting to make sure he protects her in every way a man should, including her heart when it feels this level of pain. He appreciated the art of her physical beauty, body and curves.This inspired him to want to secure his place and position at the top of this business, to make sure she is protected, never seeing a jail cell, only the finer things money can buy, even if he has to put her up in another country, to enjoy her in every way it's meant to be, giving her the reward she deserves for holding him down, being a rider. TK never envisioned or planned for this part of his takeover, when he was up state walking the yard, staring out beyond the double fences.

Suga Baby is a addition to his plans that was unexpected. Now he welcomes all of her in every way, knowing together she's not just an asset to him and this takeover, she's going to be the one that he allows into his life emotionally and mentally, giving him the much needed balance to his gangsta approach in life and this corrupt cocaine business, where loyalty and trust is limited. Right now, she is the only person he can trust to hold him down and bang out side by side if need be. TK got himself together knowing with this cartel nigga using Suga Baby's brother's phone, they need to get rid of her phone and leave this spot they're at, as soon as possible, in case he sends cartel goons their way. TK seeing first hand the magnitude of Budda's gangsta and power having her family gunned down. This only prepared him for when he discovers how his parents may have met their demise. TK didn't plan this either, for his family or innocent people that is not a part of the game to become victims. This in itself changes everything, including how he moves forward with a cold heart towards this game and all in it, because if he displays weakness outside of Suga Baby, then all of his plans for a takeover can be halted, compromised with this weak link, exposing and making him vulnerable. This is not an option he's even willing to entertain. Especially having plans to dump the thirty bricks he robbed from Big Butch, plus cop more to increase his money and power, before he heads back north for the takeover he planned for the city of Harrisburg then expand throughout the state and Tri-State area, making his presence in the game known and respected. Anyone in the way of this takeover and expansion will regret it once he set eyes on them, leaving them where the stand, in a puddle of their own blood, just to send a message to anyone else who was even thinking about doing the same thing...

Chapter 12

6:01PM Local and national news outlets are covering the story of another church shooting involving the Reverend Tracy King Senior and his wife Sister Nancy King. "I don't know who did this, but God doesn't like ugly or anyone who rises up against His children. You can run but God will still see you and the sins you have committed". A elder woman from the church said to the news cameras that wanted to speak with members of the church and the community. The massive crowd showing up rise, rage and support for the Reverend his wife and the church. As the footage of this crime is unfolding, it is also overshadowing the double homicide around the corner with Suga Baby's family, where Detectives Ritter and Wilson are. "That girl really pissed someone off, for her mother and brother to be gunned down like this". Detective Ritter said looking on at the over kill of each victim with dozens of slugs in their face and body. "You think Tony Black did this?" Detective Wilson asked. "We'll bring him in since he thinks this shit is a game of murder. We'll see how much of a game he participated in". "We can check with the company to see what the door camera caught, meaning who came in and who left ". Detective Ritter suggested. "Whoever did this, was more likely welcomed into the home. Look at the positions of the bodies, by the steps. If it was robbery or a hit, they would be dead at the front door". Detective Wilson said. "Which is even more reason to check the doorbell camera to see who was welcomed in, gunning them down". Detective Ritter responded, taking his cell phone out calling his superior at the station, to secure a warrant for the doorbell camera footage. "Ritter you'll have all the images sent to your phone within the hour". Captain Tressler said. "Thank you sir". He said ending the call, excited about being a step closer to figuring this case out. The detectives cleared the house looking up stairs coming back down, nothing in the home was disturbed.

"We're done here, we can let these guys wrap the scene up". Detective Wilson said exiting the house, seeing a small crowd has gathered, a few reporters, even fearful neighbors, especially with the shooting at the church and now this. This level of crime and violence doesn't occur in this area as it does on the other side of the Hill. Reporters and bloggers tossing questions out to the detectives, wanting answers to these brutal crimes. "Detectives, is this double homicide connected to the two at the church?" "Detectives do you have any suspects?" The detectives ignoring the questions until they have more to go on. They got into the Chevy Impala, then Detective Wilson spotted T-Black on the edge of the crowd. "I can't believe this shit". Detective Wilson said opening the car door up, jumping out, walking over to T-Black. T-Black took off running fast. This sudden action of sprinting sent a dose of adrenaline rushing through Detective Wilson, making him run after him. Detective Ritter seeing the direction he's running, started the car up, flipping the lights and siren on, taking off. T-Black running, since he's strapped, knowing the cops may think he had something to do with the shooting, when he didn't. He came to put work in, but somebody beat him to it. "Stop! Stop or I'll blow your fucking head off!" Detective Wilson yelled out running fast with his side arm in hand. T-Black also having the long barrel nickel plated .357magnum, with Rhino hollow point tips. T-Black turning into the alleyway trying to evade capture, also to find a spot to toss his weapon. "I told you to stop mutha fucka!" Detective Wilson shouted as he turned behind T-Black into the alleyway, taking aim at T-Black, firing a round. The slug whizzed pass his head. He could feel the heat of the bullet passing by. This also put into perspectives, this bitch ass cop is trying to kill me. T-Black is thinking, in fear, so he turned with the .357magnum firing off multiple thunderous shots, roaring through the air, slamming into the detective halting his forward progress abruptly, knocking the wind out of him, breaching his bullet proof vest. He slammed down hard on the ground, eyes wide in fear of this compromise to his vest, feeling pain of the slugs. He struggled to breathe from the powerful slugs crashing into his chest. T-Black turned back around to see Detective Ritter turning into the alleyway, mashing the gas racing towards him, seeing his downed partner. "Mutha fucker!" Detective Ritter said, seeing his downed partner, along with this ass hole that shot him. T-Black jumped the fence into someone's back yard, running out the other side, evading capture and the wrath of Detective Ritter who is pissed seeing his wounded partner. Detective Ritter jumping out of his car rushing over to his partner seeing the fear in his eyes, knowing shit just went terribly wrong. Detective Ritter also seeing this with the massive imprint and holes the .357magnum with Rhino slugs made. He radioed in. "This is Detective Ritter in the fifteen hundred block of North Street. I have a officer down. Shots fired! Officer down!" He shouted over the radio, along with the description of the shooter, before tending to his partner. "Look at me partner, everything is going to be okay. We'll get you fixed up so you can get that piece of shit for shooting you". Detective Ritter said trying to keep his partner alert, along with giving him comfort and confidence of things being better. The police officers came fast responding to the call, before searching for the suspect. The medics also came quick taking him away. At the same time the city is looking for T-Black along with all of his known addresses and hangouts, only to come up empty handed for now, however Detective Ritter doesn't plan on resting or giving up on his pursuit to get his partner's shooter, until he is tracked down, day and night, making it hard for T-Black to hide or get comfortable trying to sleep...

Chapter 13

Down Atlanta, TK and Suga Baby are preparing for the night, after a long day of securing a room, new phones, food, clothes and a rental car from Custom Imports. A car rental spot with Lamborghinis, Ferrari, Maybach, Bentley's, Bugatti and more, all custom painted, tricked out with the latest tech and car amenities. TK grabbed the new CLS 65 AMG Mercedes Benz, marble white with mirror tint so the haters can look at themselves watching a boss nigga and his queen. Suga Baby treated herself to diamond earrings, a diamond necklace with a crown, matching the one TK bought, on his studded chain, flowing with his diamond Brietling. All to feel good and look good, so they can assert themselves into the ATL elite, bosses, rappers of the hood and city. TK is wearing the exclusive Drake Jordan's, in Carolina Blue limited edition, with white Ralph Lauren jeans and Carolina blue button up shirt by RL, exposing his chest and chain. Suga Baby feeling and looking sexy in her six inch Cavali pumps, flowing with her red Dolce & Gabbana short dress slightly above the thigh, showing off her smooth legs and curves, up to her perky breast adding visual art in this tight dress, nipples tweaked for those taking in the art of her beauty. Even her red lipstick making her lips look kissable, with light makeup adding to her female boss look. "You look sexy as a mutha fucka. If we wasn't about to go handle business, I would put it down on ya". TK said tapping Suga Baby's ass as they're exiting the suite he got at the Marriott. "Don't tempt me, or I'll have to change this dress". She said wanting him just as much as he desired her. Their physical chemistry is explosive, coupled by the fact they really fuck with one another's gangsta side like that too. "The night is still young". TK said as they walk to the elevator getting inside. She held his hand looking up at him. "Let's make these ATL niggas respect us and what we bring". She said kissing his lips. He palmed her ass, stimulating her body always welcoming his touch. She pulled back from the kiss. "I would let you pop me inside the elevator, then again, when we come back tonight, we can start inside here and work our way to the bed". She said making him hard at the thought of this adventurous act. She looked down patting his stiffness. " I'll see you later". She said to his dick, rubbing it through his pants. He laughed feeling this pretty, sexy ass thugged out bitch. "Now let's focus". "I'm focused, it look like you got distracted". TK said as the elevator doors parted. They made their way to the CLS 65 AMG Benz. He opened the door for her, being a gangsta and a gentleman. She's warmed by the gesture, since he didn't do it before. "We taking a hundred racks in the club, plus we doing VIP and bottles. When the sparklers come all eyes will follow". TK said knowing making a visual statement will get the attention of the ballas, and anyone wanting to know who they are. More important to find a connect and a outlet to off what he has and will buy. They pulled up to Diamonds Of Atlanta, the parking lot looking like a car show with all tricked out, high end cars and trucks. People standing outside of the club with no intentions of going inside with the parking lot being it's own party. Cars blasting music, women, bottles and blunts being passed around. Soon as they parked the car, getting out, they noticed two long lines. One for celebrities and ballas, the other for regular people wanting to be in the mix of all the fame and money inside. "I'm not waiting in no line with these heels on". Suga Baby said looking on at the women dressed up ready to be chosen or be in the presence of a hood star or rapper. "Don't worry baby girl, I got this. We going to make a statement starting with the entry". TK said peeling two bands off the ten grand block He got ten in each pocket, plus twenty on his waist line. Suga Baby has the rest in her hand bag. Soon as they came up on the line, big six foot four black security guard noticed them. "Respect the line playa". TK raised the two racks up. "I don't do lines. This is for you to respect my entry. I came to play. I need VIP and bottles". TK said showing the security his pockets and waistline. He couldn't turn this serious big spender away. "Come on in playa. I got you". He said taking and tucking the two racks, before calling in over the earpiece. "We got one coming in ready to play, VIP status". The security said relaying over the radio to the female that greeted TK and Suga Baby soon as they entered. She was dressed in black lingerie. "Welcome to Diamonds Of Atlanta, I'm Drea I'll be taking you to your VIP. What will you be drinking?" "Two magnums of Ciroc. Send girls too". TK responded. "Don't worry, they'll come with the fireworks and drinks". Drea said referring to the lights and sparklers. Usually a half dozen women all looking exotic like they're coming from a photo shoot of Kite DM Magazine. Drea took them to their VIP that sits up four feet off the floor over looking the club space, stripper poles and the stages. Suga Baby looking on at the sexy ass females working their magic on the poles, dance floor with and for men and women, while being showered with money. "Drea I want to make it flood in this bitch tonight". TK said removing the sixty thousand, he took ten from Suga Baby, handed it all to Drea. " Hit me with some dollar bills. The other ten stacks is for bottles, keep them coming". Drea smiling at TK feeling his energy and excitement, then she smiled at Suga Baby to show respect. Drea walk away to fulfill his request. "She want to fuck you". Suga Baby said with the way she was looking at TK. "Nah, money and lots of it gets her wet". TK responded, pulling Suga Baby close for a kiss, palming her ass. "Now a kiss like that, I know you want to fuck me". He said making her laugh, slapping lightly at his chest, gravitating towards him emotionally.

They turned around to look at the exotic women bouncing their asses, dancing in high heels, all fit and sculpted with injections and plastic surgery, making them visual masterpieces. Each of the dancers also interacting with customers whether they're celebrities or ballas, money is the only star in Diamonds Of Atlanta. "Oh shit, here comes our drinks". Suga Baby said seeing the eight females smiling and dancing as they're walking towards them, with sparklers and lights illuminating the magnums of Ciroc, along with the six trays with ten thousand ones each stacked on top. Eight of the club's baddest dancers coming through. This in itself is a statement that is going to have people looking. "This is what the fuck I'm talking about". TK said as the smiling beauties came up with drinks and the trays of money placing them on the tables. The ladies filling up glasses serving drinks. TK taking stacks of money handing each female a thousand. "We about to have some real fun up in this bitch". "Yes we are". The females seem to chime collectively. The dancers taking TK and Suga Baby's hand leading them to the couch giving them lap dances. TK didn't have to worry about the stacks of money being stolen, the women here make that much on a good night, and this is one of them, that's why they're all here, looking sexy as ever, dancing, talking and being the best at what they do, getting to the bag. The dancers are gyrating, grinding, caressing, breathing sensual up against TK and Suga Baby. Their faces coming close and intimate, they can smell the sweetness of their expensive perfumes. Their hands even sliding across their bodies adding to the erotic lap dance. The exotic dancer with Suga Baby is Red Rain, standing five foot ten, a social media influencer, a top dancer at the club, a biracial beauty being light skinned, red hair, hazel green eyes, that seem to glow and sparkle under the lights. Perfect 38d breast she paid for, a ass sculpted to perfection, thanks to injections and exercise. Red Rain, turned around grinding her ass on Suga Baby before standing up touching her toes, twerking her ass, parting her cheeks, giving Suga Baby a glimpse of her pretty paradise. Red Rain looking back at Suga Baby making a connection to get that tip, at the same time, if she wanted to, she would fuck Suga Baby, with her sexy ass smile and dimples. Red Rain turned back around parting Suga Baby's legs, her hands sliding up her thighs, getting close to her place of passion, then she stopped, coming close allowing her breast to caress Suga Baby's face. Suga Baby stuck her tongue out touching the tip of Red Rain's nipple. "Not here, they don't play that". Red Rain said to Suga Baby, feeling her and would let her lick more than her nipples outside of the club. " I'm here all night, when you leave if you still want to get down, we can". Red Rain added before ending the dance so the other females can get their shine and coin. Suga Baby grabbed another thousand giving it to Red Rain."Next dance is on me". Red Rain said taking the stack, and a drink of the Ciroc, since there is plenty of it. The females would stay until the money and drinks are all gone. Suga Baby glanced over at TK seeing he has two dancers with him. One is grinding on him while the other is in his ear and talking. TK is in business mode networking trying to find a plug along with a connection to the hood to dump the thirty kilos he took from Big Butch. Suga Baby took a stack of money tossing it into the air to rain on the dancers who all deserved it working their magic, catering to them keeping their cups filled. Feeling the buzz of the multiple shots, Suga Baby got up dancing with the females twerking and grinding up on them. Red Rain seeing she's a wild one, that stands out to her, more than other females that came to the club with their dude or other females. The dancer TK was talking to exited the VIP to go holla at someone she know that's in position.

She went to holla at this nigga Rolo a real hood boss raised in the Thomasville Projects until he made it out, only time he looks back is to supply the hood. The dancer came back with Rolo introducing him and TK. "Rolo this is the hustla nigga TK from up north. TK this is the big hommie Rolo". Coco Brown the stripper said. Coco a sexy creature with flowing chocolate skin, voluptuous glossy lips, dimples in her smile, cat like eyes that are brown luring one in. Small waist, thick thighs and fat ass that swallows a G-string, also filled with injections. 36C implants, long jet black hair, clearly a expensive hair piece adding to her allure and exotic look. "What up folk? Shawty say you about that life. My question, is what can you do for me, if I'm already rolling?" Rolo said. Rolo standing six foot even, slim built, flashy nigga iced out, platinum watch, chains, teeth, with ice in his grill. Hair cut close with a bald fade on the sides, flowing with his baby face look. "Have a drink with me my nigga, so I can put you up on game". TK said extending his glass to be refilled by the dancers. Rolo's goons standing at the bottom of the VIP. "Get to it folk, I came to have fun tonight, not business, until Coco convince me to see what it do". "I want to buy and move a lot of work. What's your number on a block?" Rolo drowning the double shot extending for it to be refilled. "With this Ukrainian war shit popping off, gas prices is up, which is making the transport more expensive. What use to be seventeen is twenty. Anything less, is not a conversation I want to have". Rolo said being business minded, set on his number. "I need fifty of grade A only, no footprints on that shit". TK said referring to the product being cut. He removed his phone displaying the number to Rolo.

"Call me when you're ready, my money is already counted". TK said standing up to get Drea's attention. She came over. "What can I do for you? " "Get him a bottle of Ace of Spades on me".

TK said then added "This is a business gesture". Rolo dapping TK up. "You'll hear from me within twenty four hours ". "Say less". TK responded taking a hand full of money showering the dancers in VIP. Suga Baby came over to him seeing Rolo exiting with his goons. "We good?" She asked. "For now, if he is who he say he is. If he ain't, we downing him and that pretty bitch Coco". TK said drinking the shot in his hand, while cuffing Suga Baby's ass with the other hand. "Can she come back with us at the end of the night?" Suga Baby asked looking over at Red Rain dancing, as she's looking back at her biting her lip in a salacious manner. TK having a smirk on his face looking at Suga Baby then to Red Rain. "If it makes you happy, I'm game for the show, watching it go down". He responded tossing money in the air. Red Rain dropped it low going into a split, bouncing her ass up and down humping the floor, looking at Suga Baby. Suga Baby taking two hand fulls of money coming over to Red Rain. "You a bad bitch, I can't wait until tonight, he said you can come with us". Suga Baby said showering Red Rain, before tossing the remaining of the money in her hand over the other females, excited about tonight and the fact they both got what they came for, business, power and pleasure.

Chapter 14

10:01AM The next morning, breakfast is being delivered to the suite that overlooks the Atlanta skyline. TK brought the food in over to the table. He looked over at Red Rain and Suga Baby sleeping in the nude after a long intimate erotic night of sex between one another, while he enjoyed the show until Suga Baby brought him into the mix, teasing Red Rain with his length and thickness, however not allowing her to have it, only oral. This added to the level of excitement between them to be so close, involved and intimate. TK didn't trip on not being able to fuck Red Rain, she was Suga Baby's treat anyway. Now the two of them looking like art laying there sleep, still sexy as ever, with their legs intertwined for comfort, showing the curves of their bodies. He came over to the bed placing his hand on Red Rain's ass tapping it lightly until she opened her eyes. "Breakfast is ready. I know you worked up a appetite after last night". TK said, Red Rain smiling. "It was good work, her tongue had me spinning and super soaked. She a bad bitch for real". Red Rain said placing kisses on Suga Baby's lips as her free hand went down sliding over her clitoris, into her place of warmth and passion. Suga Baby's eyes opened as her body awoke to Red Rain's touch. "Mmmh, is this your way of saying good morning?" Suga Baby asked turned on, appreciating the wakeup call. Red Rain removing her finger placing it in her mouth, sucking it in a seductive manner, then removed it. "It's breakfast time". Red Rain said leaning in kissing her lips before sliding out of the bed walking over to the table of food. Suga Baby followed. They sat enjoying the eggs, bacon, scrapple, fried chicken and waffles, orange juice to chase it all down, while talking. Suga Baby is feeling Red Rain, wanting her to stick around longer so she can have more fun like last night. She just need to run it by TK. "Babe, can our new friend stick around if she likes?" Suga Baby tossed out there looking at her.

Red Rain caught off guard yet appreciating the gesture. TK looked at Red Rain, yes she's exotic looking, a go getta, but is she really about this life we living? He's thinking, while chewing his chicken and waffles. "Last night was fun, no doubt. This life me and baby girl living isn't all fun. It's about violence and power". TK stated reaching for his orange juice to chase his food down, then looking at Red Rain, to see how she absorbed his words. She paused from her eggs and bacon feeling a way about how he views her as if she isn't about that life because she's sexy. "Is that suppose to push me away or scare me off?" Red Rain said sitting her fork down then added. "I've been around that shit all my life". She stood from the table turning her nude body to the side showing the pattern of roses tattooed on her left ass cheek. " You probably didn't notice, I got shot in my ass, holding a nigga down. The tattoo covers the scar". TK looked over at Suga Baby who is smiling ear to ear. "She's a rida just like me babe". Suga Baby said looking at Red Rain. Before TK could respond his cell phone sounded off. He already knew it is Rolo, since the only other person with his number is sitting at the table. "Yo what's good with you?!" TK said. "You already known folk. Say man, around twelve I'll be at the hommie's rim spot on Peach Tree". "I'll be there". TK said ending the call then asked Red Rain. "You know where the rim shop on Peach Tree is?" "Yeah that's where all the ballas go to support the rap legend's spot, plus a lot of rappers hang out there". "We have to be there at twelve, y'all need to jump in the shower and get ready. Suga Baby stay focus, we have to get this paper ". He said knowing the two of them be on freaky time. They walk to the shower, he looked on at how priceless the view of them is. He got up checking the money, making sure it's a mil, even. TK is so focused on the take over of the north and here in ATL with the supply of product coming in.

While they got in the shower, TK got dressed having took a shower soon as he got up, like he on jail time waking up 6AM like he has to stand for count. This early to rise routine, also kept him on point, reminding him to stick to the script of his plans he laid out for this future of money and power. Now he has this new edition in Red Rain wanting to be down. Craving more than the excitement of sex, wanting to be a part of the process of this takeover. Little do she know, this isn't all about fucking, sucking and licking, it's real. She going to have to put some work in to prove herself to him. He don't need just a pretty face to stick around. He can find one of those in every city across the nation. He needs a rida like Tati was and Suga Baby is. Anything less will be moved to the side, out of the way of what he and Suga Baby is doing. Within the hour the ladies was ready looking the part of two sexy ass boss bitches, strapped up with guns Suga Baby gave to Red Rain to make sure shit went smoothly with Rolo. TK didn't trust many, because that shit cost too much. So he stayed on point, even dealing with this nigga that has more than him, in case hard times fall on him. Not that it's the case today, TK thought everything through. "Rain since you know where we going you can drive". TK said tossing her the keys. " Then added, if anything looks out of place or you think something is wrong, make it known by using that gun Suga Baby gave you". TK added. "Like I said I'm no stranger to this life style". Red Rain responded popping the clip out of the .45 Automatic, checking the rounds, before slamming the clip

94

back into the gun, chambering a round, flipping the safety off. "No need for the safety when you have a ready mindset". Red Rain stated giving TK a brief smile displaying her sexy lady gangsta. He didn't respond other than leading the way to take care of this business, feeling this new edition in Red Rain, especially if she's as deadly as she's exotic.

Chapter 15

Up north in Harrisburg, Pennsylvania; Homicide Detective Ritter found out where T-Black is laid up, at his girlfriend's crib on Moore Murder, a street in the uptown area of the city, known for heavy drug traffic and violent shoot outs. This info came from one of his CIs relaying this info. Detective Ritter taking the shooting of his partner personal, so he didn't call for back up. He parked his car around the corner, walking to the address he was given. He walked pass a few drug dealers trapping, they weren't his focus, he was tuned in to one thing. Seeking out this piece of shit that shot his partner, that is in bad condition from the Rhino slugs that breached his vest. Detective Ritter closed in on 2139 Moore Street, coming to the door, taking a deep breath to calm himself for what he has in store. He looked around, no one is paying him any attention being focused on their own illegal business. He came up to the door covering the peep hole, before knocking on the door. A few minutes later a female voice came from the other side of the door. "Who is it?" She asked trying to look through the peep hole that's blacked out. Detective Ritter is silent, processing his thoughts along with his next move of crossing the line, that he can never come back from, making him a criminal like the ones he pursues daily. "Whoever it is, you better move your finger from the peep hole or I'm not opening the door!" She added, getting upset, standing firm. This also got T-Black's attention, making him come down stairs to the door with his gun in hand. "Who the fuck is it!?" T-Black asked. Right then Detective Ritter zeroed in on the familiar male voice, removing his finger from the peep hole, at the same time T-Black is looking through the peep hole. In one swift motion, locked in on the last location of the male voice, Detective Ritter placed his gun to the peep hole squeezing off all seventeen rounds through the peep hole and door, crashing into T-Black's face and body, snapping his head back with brute force, ejecting chunks of skull and brains out the other side, followed by pounding slugs tearing into his flesh over and over sucking the thugged out life from his body. The slugs, blood spatter and brain matter, spraying and hitting the female, dropping her, leaving her wounded. Detective Ritter now pumped up from the rush of unloading the entire clip through the door, he took off running, heart pounding, mind racing knowing he just crossed the line and the point of no return. He's a murderer, but it feels so good to him for having avenged his partner. "What are you looking at!?" He yelled out pointing his empty gun at the

The Crown Is Mine

young hustlas, they took cover just as the rest of those out, when they heard the multiple gun shots being fired. No one want to be shot by accident in being nosey trying to see what's going on. Detective Ritter making it to his car breathing hard, his lungs burning from the fast sprint, never having ran like this. "Yeah! I got you mutha fucka! That's for you partner!" Detective Ritter said starting his car, mashing the gas taking off, knowing he has to think ahead now, because soon he too would be running for his life and freedom, once they discover it was a homicide detective that committed this crime of violence against a police shooting suspect. In this very moment for him, it was all worth it, the way he feels, pumped up, adrenaline flowing just as fast as his heart is beating and his mind is racing. The level of endorphins induced into his mind giving him the rush of murder most serial killers have, enjoying taking life. He raced through the uptown streets hearing sirens blaring going towards the area he just left from. "He dead! Ain't no need to rush boys!" Detectives Ritter yelled feeling himself and this act of murder that made him a criminal. " He shot the wrong one this time!" He added having done his research on T-Black seeing that he had shot at cops before, but never again.

Detective Ritter raced through the city heading to his house outside of the city, where he sat in the drive way still revved up, thinking about what he just did. At the same time, a part of him realizing he just ruined all he stood for as a homicide detective, a officer of the law, along with being a husband and a father. If they ever discovered he's the shooter for this, he wouldn't go quiet. A person of his stature having sent many men and women to prison for murder and other crimes. These criminals would have their way with him, before they would eventually kill him for locking them up. Detective Ritter trying to calm his mind to think ahead of this thing. Now has thoughts of taking his wife and kid to a non extradition country where they could live without the worry of prosecution. The hardest part of this would be trying to convince his wife of this, who isn't fond of being far from her family, especially her aging mother and father. Just as he was preparing to go into the house, it came over the radio a cop shot Tony Black and female at the residence in the uptown area. The spike in adrenaline rushing through his body, when he entered the home trying to get his wife to leave with him, and he would explain it all later. She didn't want to leave, because of how he was conducting himself outside of the person she's known all these years. The look in his eyes are even different with the rush of murder still lingering in his eyes. "Okay I'll be back. I have to stop at the hospital to see my partner off. Then I'll be back when things settle down". Detective Ritter said hyped up, his mind is racing just as fast as his heart. " What? What does that even mean?" She questioned as he hurried back out to his car, knowing it's a

The Crown Is Mine

matter of time before they come to his house. He didn't want to be here when they come, so he took off pumped up, not really knowing what his next move is, however he did know the protocol the police would use to track him.

Chapter 16

Five and half weeks later, TK, Suga Baby and Red Rain managed to off load the eighty kilos, throughout the ATL, ballas coming from other states along with sending Red Rain to PA, to connect with the streets of Harrisburg, York, Philly, Allentown, Reading, and Lancaster. All made possible through Red Rain's Followers on Instagram, that slid into her DM. She picked out the real ballas and go gettas, tapping into them, working her magic. They all wanted to fuck her, so they got down with the hopes they would one day get a chance, plus the numbers she was giving them is better than what they was getting. TK also put Coco Brown down with the team. She's responsible for connecting with the hood of ATL. She put Trappa-D and Little Ki Ki from Bank Head on. Trappa-D a five foot ten, eighteen year old dark skin nigga with braids, black colored eyes, medium built, gold fronts, a real street nigga about his money. Trappa-D's hommie Little Ki Ki, she a Tomboy thugged out chick, only nineteen, with dreadlocks that reach her shoulders, always dressing like a nigga, Timberland boots, jeans, sports jersey, baseball cap, with her 10mm

Colt tucked under the jersey. The light skinned Tomboy thug even has a raspy cadence of a dude. She got more bitches than most niggas too, just as she got more money than them. She didn't play when it came down to chasing this paper. She would lay a nigga down and still look to be paid by mutha fuckas they hung around or they would get it too. TK having met the ATL playas getting their respect and loyalty, along with the power he sought after. At the same time, Eguardo 'Budda' Sanchez, used his federal and street resources to track the phone that Suga Baby once used to contact her baby brother. The cell phone towers last known use, pinged it here in Atlanta. It directed him here in Atlanta, then he used his street resources to track them, in discovering a new player buying and distributing large sums of cocaine. Budda being the distributor of the northeast, as for the Southeast, that is ran by cartel Capo, Rosanna 'La Vieja' Santiago. A fifty two year old Mexicana, from Juarez, now residing in Miami, Florida. The five foot even, one hundred and twenty pound boss, with dark eyes, stare, black curly hair that stops at her shoulders, made her bones back home, rising through the ranks, becoming a capo in the cartel and a bread winner for the business, moving more cocaine than anyone else in America. Budda having contacted her, discovered large sums going into ATL. He noticed this also trickled up north cutting into his business. Budda and his four goons pulled up on the Soul

Food restaurant, where he had his associates track TK and his team to; Suga Baby, Coco Brown, Red Rain, Little Ki Ki, Trappa-D was all enjoying the soul food buffet of collard greens, bake macaroni, string beans, ribs, chicken wings, fried fish, chittlings, blueberry cornbread, butter milk biscuits, with freshly squeezed lemonade to chase it all down. For TK this is his family of ridas. Soon as the two Range Rovers pulled up outside, the young goons from Little Ki Ki and Trappa-D's projects became alert, keeping eyes on them. Budda's two goons entered first followed by him, then the other two came behind him. "OG who these Spanish niggas coming through?" Little Ki Ki asked one hand on her chicken wing the other on her 10mm Colt that's on her lap. Trappa-D did the same thing, seeing the seriousness on their faces as they closed in on their table. TK put his pork chop down, licking his fingers, reaching to his right to remove his nickel plated snub nose .44magnum, holding it down pulling the hammer back, ready to rock out. Both TK and Suga Baby noticing the face of Budda from the video call. Suga Baby jumped up quick removing her weapon, at the same time Budda's goons whipped out their guns. The two behind him came to the front to protect him. Everybody at the table now standing revealing their guns, ready to go all out.

"Don't do this in my restaurant". The owner yelled out. "Shut the fuck up, this is personal shit!" Suga Baby snapped. "I'll gun all you mutha fuckas down to get to his bitch ass!" She added. The young project niggas outside came in, guns at the ready, hearing all the commotion going on. Now Budda having young thugs with no care for life standing behind him and his men, trapped in between them. "I'm a federal agent. You shoot or kill me, you're all going down!" He tried to plea using the cop card, knowing he has no way out. This didn't go as he expected it, to come in her and gun them down or scare them into giving him his millions. "You crossed that line when you killed my mom and dad, in their church making you the Devil himself". TK said. "Devil or not hermano, I have a badge. You kill a federal agent, you and your friends go to death row". TK came around the table, walking over to Budda. His goons shifting their weapons on TK, as he approaches. "You came here to get your money and kill me and my girl. If I let you walk out, next time we may not be so lucky to see you coming. At this point, your badge of being a federal agent is tainted with the blood of the people you murdered. I hope that queen bitch was worth it". TK said lowering his weapon, then added. " Take this mutha fucka and his flunkies outside to show the owner some respect ". They all closed in on them, placing guns to their faces. The Mexican goons not going out like that, so they shift their weapons to TK since he's the boss. TK fired the powerful magnum sending massive slugs crashing into their bodies, along with the others firing on these Mexican goons. At the same time Budda tried to flee making it outside until the project niggas shot him in the back and legs dropping him. Suga Baby ran over to the downed Budda as he turned over he faced her deadly beauty as she stared down at him, she squatted down placing her gun to his temple.

"This is for my mom and baby bro, you piece of shit". She said squeezing the trigger, blowing his brains out on the sidewalk, giving her the self gratification and revenge she wanted from the moment he step foot into her mom's house, posing a threat and killing her mom and baby brother. TK looking back at the owner giving him this murderous look, that means don't say a word. "Don't worry my nigga, I'll take care of you". They all left the scene knowing everything is about to change for them, good and bad. Good meaning they don't have to worry about this crooked FBI agent slash cartel Lieutenant and murderer, chasing behind them. Good meaning, they could go back north locking shit down in the city and Northeast with him no longer in the picture for distribution. Bad meaning, this crooked federal agent still will be honored as a officer of the law. So the federal government will go hard trying to find his killer by any means necessary. Even with them not being aware his secret life as a cartel boss and associate, living a tainted and murderous lifestyle that has lead to his own demise.

Chapter 17

For three weeks straight, the FBI, DEA, and Atlanta homicide, bombarded the streets of Atlanta, taking down drug kingpins, arms dealers and local thugs, wanting answers for the death of Federal Agent Eguardo Sanchez. The FBI's objective is to shake the tree to see what falls, meaning, to see if anyone comes forth ratting out whoever is responsible. TK and the team had shit on lock, paying the soul food restaurant owner fifty racks to keep hush about this, and he would see more money over time. All other witnesses dropped low at the sound of gunfire, not seeing anything. Suga Baby and Red Rain is in their new townhouse they got in her name. The three large bedrooms, three and a half bathrooms, marble floors and fireplace, granite counter tops in the kitchen. A study they turned into a makeshift vault with boxes and bags of money. A lower level game, lounge and entertainment area, with a stripper pole. Something Red Rain had installed, keeping the excitement between her and Suga Baby going. They also had the plush towne home outfitted with cameras securing the back and front entrances. The make shift vault also having guns spread out for quick access, if shit hit the fan while they was in their counting money. They also had one gun in each room, even though the ladies slept with TK most nights. TK is in the kitchen with Red Rain and Suga Baby watching them put their chef skills to use. "It smells good and looks good from here". TK said looking at their fat asses as they stood by the stove and counter top. "It taste good too". Red Rain said looking over her shoulder at TK flirting with him. He smiled knowing she's talking about her pink pocket, that loves his tongue work. His cell phone sounded off, it's Rolo. Something must be up. He just grabbed a hundred, it wasn't time to bounce back yet. "Yo what's good?" "Say man, I got that for ya man". Rolo responded, sounding off. TK also picked up on this, becoming alert. He put the phone on speaker so the girls can hear this nigga. "Yo my nigga, you off beat a little, feel me? That song played already". TK said speaking in code. "So you want me to bring it to you or what? I got a hundred of them things for the low". Rolo said sounding like he's under pressure. TK hung up quick, taking the battery and sim card out of his phone. "The feds or somebody got to this nigga, he trippen". TK said at the same time Red Rain's cell phone started ringing. "It's Coco Brown, should I answer it?" Red Rain asked. "Hell no, she introduced TK to that nigga Rolo. That bitch and Rolo got compromised, now they trying to taken us down with them". Suga Baby said. "Take the sim cards and batteries out of y'all phones. Anyone Coco knows about, we shut them out until we see if they got turned. Get dressed, we leaving to toss these phones and get new ones". TK said. Coco nor Rolo knew about the townhouse, so they good on that end of things. TK pissed that the nigga who supplies him is trying to take him down. Big fish eat little fish type shit. That stupid mutha fucka knew the feds and cops was storming the streets, making sweeps, and he should move quiet, be mindful of who you bring into your circle. He fucked up allowing himself to be compromised. While TK and the ladies moved smart to stay ahead of the game and the feds. On the other side of Atlanta, the DEA has Rolo and Coco Brown in custody, squeezing them for information. "One hundred and fifty kilos, over a dozen guns and assault rifles that's modified, with no serial numbers, two million in cash. Huh, between the two of you, means life with no parole. Not unless you can give us something, a name or names of who is responsible for killing federal Agent Sanchez". Agent Brian Tucker stated firmly staring at Rolo and Coco Brown wanting them to break. Coco never told Rolo about her being present that day at the shooting. She never even spoke about it after that day, knowing what it could bring. Coco also knowing, having in debt knowledge of this could put her on federal death row, getting the gas chamber. She didn't want to suffer.

Rolo didn't know who took out the federal agent, only chatter of who may have done it. Trying to save himself from a jail cell, he tried taking TK down with him. He even convince Coco to reach out to Red Rain. "I got a lot of playas that be grabbing heavy from me. Is that what you want?" "You are stupid. We don't go low, we go high, meaning give us the shooter of Federal Agent Sanchez, or give us the person who supplies you, and we'll see that you walk free. If you don't have anything to give us, then you can kiss your ass and the streets of Atlanta goodbye". Agent Tucker said. Rolo fearing the worse of being taken from this balla lifestyle of having it all. "I can give you my connect, but I can't spend a day in jail, because they'll kill me". Rolo said knowing they have a long reach of contracted gang assassins. "Now that's what I'm talking about, dead man walking". Agent Tucker taunted, knowing Rolo's a dead man either way, unless he opts for witness protection. "Now what do you have for us?" Agent Tucker asked Coco. "I know this bitch running around here wanted for homicide up north". Coco said, talking about Suga Baby, having seen a old picture of Suga Baby with Wanted under her name and face on social media. Suga Baby's new look didn't fool her, she just never said anything about it being from the hood, honoring the street code up until now. "Homicide huh?" Agent Tucker said looking at Coco Brown, then over to Rolo. "You should be like her, she got a homicide to talk about. Only if you could tell us about Agent Sanchez". "I told you I don't know nothing about that shit. What I got is a cartel capo. You want this info or what man? I can't be sitting here all day, people gone start looking for me". Agent Tucker sat down, sliding two writing tablets across the table with two pens. "I want names, numbers and details, then we'll go from there".

Agent Tucker said. Rolo gave them all the information needed, drop times, usual quantity he purchases and more. Even calling La Vieja scheduling a re-up. Coco Brown, wrote down the details of Suga Baby's new look, where she be at, how she moves product and to whom. She didn't have knowledge of the homicide, she expressed only that Suga Baby was on the run from Pennsylvania, wanted for murderer. The two of them Rolo and Coco turning their backs on the street code along with the same people who would have held them down, while they're locked up, never wanting for anything. Even their families would have been taken care of, now they put it all on the line to evade a jail cell, like they didn't know this lifestyle they're living came with that risk of prison, getting robbed or murdered. Now Rolo and Coco are rats, having turned into federal and state witnesses. At the same time putting a target on themselves and maybe all they love if the cartel capo, and Suga Baby can't get to them, before the FBI puts them in federal witness protection. Both Coco and Rolo turned their backs on the streets and people that would have held them down to their last breath. Now they both know their actions, changes the course of how their lives will play out, making them look over their shoulders forever.

Chapter 18

A month after Rolo and Coco Brown's betrayal, caught up with them. The two knowing the heat from the streets would come down along with the cartel capo he betrayed, Rosanna 'La Vieja' Santiago. The cartel capo posting a two million dollar cash bail, having legal businesses that cut the check. Now the powerful cartel affiliate set out to make an example out of Rolo and the bitch Coco Brown that was at his side when they pretended to be buying the large shipment of cocaine. The message and statement was not only made known public, it made national news for its Mexican cartel style killing. "Babe turn to News Nation". Suga Baby said coming down stairs where TK and Red Rain is sitting on the couch snuggled up against him. Suga Baby condoned it since they're all in a relationship together, making them bonded more than family. They would ride and die for each other. Suga Baby came over sitting on the other side, taking the remote tuning into News Nation. Dan Abraham's show is on. "The footage you're about to see is graphic, so if there are children around please remove them". Dan Abraham said before the video footage rolled, he described the content being shown. "The federal agents say this cartel style decapitation and hanging of the bodies from the feet, is to make a statement against anyone who has betrayed the loyalty of the cartel". Dan said. The female and male body having their heads cut off, hanging from the bridge in the city where all passing by would see. "The FBI has reported that the heads of these two victims where mailed to the Bureau of Investigations, also sending a message to the FBI for flipping these two individuals into ratting as they say in the streets. The two victims as reported are Roland 'Rolo' Patterson, and Lori 'Coco Brown' Myers. The FBI has reported they'll be looking into this case that attempted to halt their investigation of drug trafficking and murders. I'm Dan Abraham's, tune in later for more on this story".

Suga Baby and Red Rain looking on at TK feeling a sense of relief the cartel got this nigga and that bitch. "Now that they're out of the way, we still need to find a new plug with the product running low". Red Rain said, wanting to keep the north on lock down. "I'll figure something out, even if we have to go to Texas, network close to the border to see what we come up with". TK said. "Or we can vacation down in Mexico to find a plug?" Suga Baby said wanting to have fun, show off her body and network all at the same time. "It ain't that easy in Mexico, to go down there flashy looking like a million.

We'll end up buried in the hills of Juarez. We have to pace ourselves and be smart about the process. Everything will fall into place. Plus we have to stay on point for these feds still searching for someone to take that bitch ass agent's body". TK said. His cell phone sounded off. It's Little Ki Ki from the hood. He trusted her and Trappa-D, they real thugs and hustlas about this street life. They respect the code of the streets. " Ki Ki what's good with you?" TK answered the phone. "Say folk, you see the news?" "Yeah that shit played out the way it was suppose to". "Karma's a bitch". Little Ki Ki laughed then added "What it do folk, the hood is hungry out here, ya feel me?" "You already know I'm not going let the little hommies starve. I'm a get at you in a little". "I'm around ya feel me?" Little Ki Ki said hanging up. "Rain, take ten up north. I know it ain't much but we down to twenty. We split ten up top ten down here". TK said trying to be strategic. "No". "No? What you mean no?" "Twenty, we dump here. I'll put the north on hold. Plus right now we need to stick together, until things start going smooth as they were". Red Rain responded making sense, while making him respect her even more, for thinking ahead, as a team player. "Let's go make that drop on Little Ki Ki and Trappa-D ". He said standing up preparing to drop a couple bricks in the hood.

Little Ki Ki be breaking the bricks down to nicks, dimes, twenties, and fifties, making close to a hundred off of each kilo, no cutting it, straight raw, making all the fiends come back. She's been had enough to cop heavy, instead she be stacking her bread, not being flashy. She got seven Nike and Timberland shoe boxes full of money. She didn't stunt out buying cars, or bling, that shit be drawing on a nigga, she feels and think. Plus she has visions, a plan for her end game, to invest the money legally. Also she be stacking to have in case shit go wrong. She'll have bail and lawyer money. Trappa-D on the other hand, he hood rich, always wanting niggas out here to see he got bread, by being a flashy boss nigga. He always be buying the bar out, taking strippers and shawties in the hood shopping. He even got gold and platinum chains, watches, rings all iced out. He got the Dodge Charger tricked out race car red, big 24inch rims, system, TVs, and hidden compartments. He got a Hiabusa 1300cc all black with red flames and chrome flakes in the custom paint. Trappa-D be in the hood Gucci down, shirt, belt, pants, glasses and watches. All to look the part while serving fiends and the little hommies in the hood that be grabbing eight balls and ounces from him. They all be excited looking up to him, plus he be giving them product lower than he should, or he would give out extra to keep them coming. All tactics that's good for business at first, but long term, that shit cuts into profits. Little Ki Ki be getting on him about that shit, but Trappa-D think she be tripping by not stunting on these niggas out here, the way they getting this money. Her thinking is long term. She also made it clear to him about how he looking out for the little hommie and fiends, as long as it doesn't start cutting into her paper and profits he can do what he wants, since he seems like he's going to do this any way. Little Ki Ki is definitely the more focused of them.

Chapter 19

TK, Suga Baby and Red Rain is in the snow white S600L Mercedes Benz, white rims, plush snow white leather seats, all custom features, TVs, system, along with other lavish amenities of this luxury vehicle. This Benz is Red Rain's gift from TK and Suga Baby for her loyalty and holding the north down. The tinted windows concealing them as they headed to the hood to link up with Trappa-D and Little Ki Ki, to drop a load off on them, to keep the hood satisfied. They're all focused on the future of this empire he's building. As they're driving over to the hood Red Rain is blasting; We Getting Money, By Sheff G. A song that had them in the zone of getting this paper. Anything less is not an option. Anyone in their way of getting this bag of money, will meet their demise. As Red Rain turned down the street heading to the hood, she spotted two young niggas ducking in between cars, sneaking along side of the cars guns out, like they about to shoot it out or get the drop on someone. "Look at these fools in broad day light". Red Rain said, slowing down in case they was about to start shooting, she didn't want her car or those inside to be caught in the crossfire. These two young niggas have been watching Little Ki Ki knowing she getting that money, even though she not flashy, they figured she stacking that paper and they want parts of it. The young goons jumped out on Little Ki Ki seeing her counting money she just got from a customer. "Say shawty run that paper ya fell feel me?" The young goon said aiming his rusty .32 automatic. The other young buck having a .25 automatic. Little Ki Ki was counting the money, looked up at these clown as niggas. She didn't fear death, knowing it came with the life style she's living. "Y'all bitch ass niggas with them little ass guns, trying to get at me and my paper!" She said with a smirk on her face, standing her ground, at the same time placing her hand on her waist line where her 10mm Colt is.

"Y'all stupid ass niggas could have gotten a blessing, if you would have asked me to put you on". She paused looking at the money in her hand, a couple hundred dollars. "This what you want, take it". She said tossing it in their faces. "This bitch is crazy". The young buck said snapping, taking his gun, pistol whipping her, knocking her Atlanta Braves baseball cap off, staggering her back, grabbing her face. She laughed seeing Red Rain and Suga Baby coming down the street on feets, guns out ready to back her up and put work in. "You bitch ass mutha fuckas should have taken the money. Now I'm a make you pay for testing my G". She said. The young niggas seeing her eyes veer pass them. They look back too late, facing the Glocks staring back at them. "What y'all stupid ass young niggas thought cause she a female out here getting money she weak?" Suga Baby said. Little Ki Ki having her 10mm Colt in hand walking up on the young nigga that hit her with the butt of his gun. She eyed him down, before slamming the butt of her gun into his face over and over again. "Agggh, agggh!" He screamed in pain, releasing his gun to grab his face, knowing if he tried to use the gun she would kill him. "Don't act like a bitch now! That shit hurt huh?" Little Ki Ki said dropping the young nigga with multiple blows to his face with the butt of her gun. He laid on the ground holding his bloody face. "And you with this little ass gun. Give me that shit". Little Ki Ki said taking the other young buck's .25 automatic. " You better be glad I got shit to take care of, or I would put a bullet in both of y'all bitch ass niggas". Little Ki Ki said picking the money up off the ground she tossed at them. "Now get the fuck out of my hood before I change my mind!" The young bucks got themselves together taking off running, feeling like bitches having botched this robbery, being exposed by this gangsta chick. Red Rain came over to Little Ki Ki caressing her face seeing the bruise from the pistol slamming into her face. "You good baby girl?" Red Rain asked. "That shit ain't about nothing, it'll heal". "You a tough bitch huh? That's what I'm talking about, outshine and out grind

these niggas. Now let's go handle our business ". Red
Rain said, respecting Little Ki Ki's gangsta. "Yo where the
fuck is Trappa-D at?" Suga Baby asked, knowing this
attempt robbery would have never happen if he was
present. The niggas know he don't play that shit. "He in
the crib breaking down the last of what we had". Little Ki
Ki responded securing her gun on her waist line, before
adjusting her Braves baseball cap. They all went inside the
crib securing the business, dropping product off and
picking money up. "What up Trappa-D? You know these
two lame ass niggas just tried to stick Little Ki Ki". Suga
Baby said sitting the bag with the kilos down on the table.
"What? Them fools trippen". Trappa-D said looking at
Little Ki Ki. "Nah they was trippen trying to get at me
with them rusty and little ass guns". Little Ki Ki said not
phased by what happened, she knows it is all a part of the
game. As far as she's concerned, them bitch ass niggas got
the worse end of it. They focused back on business giving
them the money in exchange for the product. Once they
secured that they headed back to the townhouse, trying
to figure out their next move when the last of the bricks
run out. TK was even thinking about venturing off to the
ecstasy or molly business knowing it's a hustla and club
drug that can make millions up and down the east coast.
This would keep the money coming in, giving them
power and recognition in the underground world. Either
way he can't stop here, especially having went through all

he did to achieve what he has thus far, with his team, Red Rain and Suga Baby, two ride or die females with brains, exotic looks, and a sensational appetite for power and the finer things in life.

Chapter 20

As Red Rain is pulling up to the townhouse preparing to park in the driveway. She noticed four black tinted Yukon Denalis turning the corner. "I don't know who the fuck this is, heads up y'all coming our way". She said reaching for her gun, if it's the feds they going out in a hell of gunfire, because jail is not a option for either of them. "That looks like the feds". Suga Baby said taking hold of her gun preparing for the end. The convoy of Yukon's came to a halt in front of the townhouse. Three of the truck's doors opened, men exiting. Two standing at the front of the unopened truck, two at the back on each side for security, looking real professional, but not feds as they all first thought. The other men closed in on the parked S600L Mercedes Benz, almost like they were watching all of them. "These Spanish niggas ain't feds". TK said. "It's a hit, that bitch from the cartel taking out anyone connected to Rolo and that hoe Coco". Red Rain said having her gun pressed up against the door, ready to unload. "If it was a hit, we would have never seen them coming, or they would be shooting now. Roll the window down to see what these mutha fuckas want". TK said, she obliged. "What y'all want?" Red Rain asked, still having her gun up against the door. "La Vieja wants to talk". The well dressed Mexican goon said. "Who she want to talk to?" "You sound like you're in charge bonita, pero, La Vieja wants to talk to the one in control". Red Rain rolled her eyes before turning to look at TK to see if he even wanted to have this conversation. "I'm good, this might be what we was looking for". TK said exiting the car. They walked him over to the trucks, patting him down for weapons, taking his .45 Desert Eagle off his waist, before nodding to their boss hidden behind the dark tinted windows. The back window came down releasing a cloud of smoke, from the long Virginia Slim cigarette Rosanna 'La Vieja' Santiago is smoking. The smoke dissipating revealing her face.

"Tracy King AKA TK from PA. You're a real goon and a hustla, that has taken in blood, the power he wants. It reminds me of my rise to power". La Vieja said before pausing giving him time to think about who she is and how she knows about him. "Get in, we have serious business to tend to". She added. He got in on the other side. "I know who you are now". TK said. "Then you know my serious and unlimited capabilities". "I do". "We need to keep this thing going as they were, without interruption as your previous associate attempted". She said turning to look at TK blowing a cloud of smoke out. "That mutha fucka and his bitch got what they deserve. Me and my team, we don't bend or break for no one". TK said firmly, reassuring her of his honor to the street code. "I believe you amigo. I can see it in your eyes, the hunger for more. The determination to be king of this business. Be mindful to never get ahead of yourself. Always understand who put you in power". She said puffing her cigarette then added. "I want to front you two hundred and fifty kilos on top of what you want to buy. This will allow you to secure the northeast". "What happens when you're going through that legal beef, that rat ass mutha fucka put you in?" TK asked wanting to know if he'll have a constant supply. TK bringing this up made her think about Rolo's betrayal, and having to set an example out of him, and his lady friend. It also made her angered by the fact she has to face this legal problem. With lawyers, money and postponements, she'll fend it off as long as possible, with hopes to later plea it down or flee the country. "Allow me to worry about this small matter. Nothing or no one will come between this business of ours. Anything you need, or any problems you have and can't handle. Pass them onto me, I'll make sure they no longer exist". La Vieja said looking on at TK displaying how serious and violent she is, even with her beauty, she's deadly and not to be fucked with.

"Do we have an agreement hermano?" She added. "We good. Just let me know when you're ready and where to be at to handle this business". "You'll be contacted by one of my associates, this will be the last time we speak face to face, unless something comes up that needs my time, attention and resources". She said nodding her head excusing TK. He exited the truck making his way over to the townhouse where Suga Baby and Red Rain stood at the bottom of the steps awaiting him to be done taking care of business. His walk was even different feeling this next level of power. He already has enough to grab two hundred bricks himself, plus the two fifty she going dump on him. He can change the game with giving uncut product at a better cost than most, and plenty of it. TK looked over his shoulder as he got on the side walk watching the convoy of trucks driving off. "That was the boss bitch La Vieja. She the cartel connect. She about to supply us, plus bless us with two fifty on top of what we grab". TK said. Both Red Rain and Suga Baby got excited at the sound of this, knowing it's going to give them all financial freedom and power. This level of power is turning them on in a sexual way like the dancers at Diamonds of Atlanta. "You want to celebrate this new position of power?" Suga Baby asked caressing TK's chest with one hand and Red Rain's ass with the other hand, squeezing her soft butt. "Let's go inside of the house before this freak start taking our clothes off out here". Red Rain said loving her girl Suga Baby. "Don't give me no ideas, plus people can watch, that makes it more fun". Suga Baby

The Crown Is Mine

responded as they made their way into the house to celebrate with drinks, and each other on intimate erotic levels
that will feel even better now having achieved his and
their goal of being in power being the king of this game
while having two bad ride or die females as his queens. He
now has the crown. Suga Baby and Red Rain are his diamonds to complete it all.

"You ready to have rich sex babe?" Suga Baby said to
TK being funny yet turned on by this money talk, taking
his hand leading him to the couch, ready to fuck his face
and body. Red Rain following them, coming up behind
TK caressing his back, reaching around touching his long
thick manhood. He got hard quick, feeling her soft
touch. Suga baby joining in with kisses before they
undressed him, allowing him to explore each of their
bodies with his tongue and dick, giving them erotic satis-
faction, on the couch, to the floor, legs up, spread wide,
from behind, deep and long strokes, melodic moans per-
meating through the air. Each of them falling for this
man his touch and attention to the details of knowing
their bodies and what gets them to their place of orgasmic
eruptions. A little over a hour has passed by before they
all laid side by side in sweet sweat of the flesh, glistening
feeling on top of the world having it all, with this new
position of power that will allow them to take over every
city and state from ATL to New York. What better feeling to be in power, along with having the baddest ride or

die bitches who want the same as he does. This is more than he envisioned being locked down planning for ten years. Even knowing this, his level of hunger still exist as if it's his first day out of prison. It's a must for him to stay in survival beast mode. He's thinking and feeling staring at the ceiling fan rotating. A smirk came across his face embracing the power, new position and these sexy ass ride or die bitches to share it all with.

The Crown Is Mine

Chapter 21

Close to a month passed by with Detective Ritter running for his life, as a fugitive for killing T-Black and wounding his girlfriend. The Mechanicsburg Police Department along side of Homicide detectives from Harrisburg and the SWAT team found themselves outside of Detective Ritter's home, after he went back to try to convince his wife to leave. She is in fear, now knowing he's on the run for murder. Also his enraged behavior scared her, so she called for help and they came fast ready to secure this murder suspect, disregarding he was once one of their own. This made him even more dangerous, because he knows the protocol they're going through with him being barricaded in his home, with his wife and child present. "Come out with your hands up! We have the house surrounded, there is no way out of this!" The SWAT team leader Paul Beamer yelled out. Detective Ritter is pacing back and forth from the bedroom door his wife locked herself into, to the front door of this one floor ranch style home. He can see SWAT and police officers standing along side their units, with guns at the ready. This isn't how he wanted to end his career or marriage. He couldn't bare to look at his daughter Brianna, knowing he failed as a good guy being a police officer, he failed as a husband and father in making the emotionally charged decision, to kill T-Black for shooting and wounding his partner. All because he wanted to match the level of gangsta these street thugs only respect, which is brute force and violence. Detective Ritter became even more enraged seeing that his wife locked herself into their bedroom. The level of anger and pressure of this situation is mounting by the second, and he is fully aware that the SWAT will come in and fast. Their main objective is to preserve life, while containing, and securing the threat. He is the threat to his wife and child at this point. "Loraine open this God damn door!" Detective Ritter shouted banging on the bedroom door, jolting her with fear of him coming through the door, inflicting harm or her and their daughter. Something she has not only seen in movies, but in real life watching News Nation and other media outlets. "I know you hear me Loraine! Open this mutha fucka before I start putting holes through the door!" Detective Ritter shouted, as his mind is slipping into a dark raging mental state of no point of return. His breathing is heavy, his mind and heart is racing trying to figure a way out of this. Right now his only leverage is barricaded inside of their bedroom. Loraine is sitting on the bed holding their daughter in between her legs close

The Crown Is Mine

to to her. Brianna is scared and crying wondering why her father is so loud and sounding angry. The 911 operator can also hear the commotion, relaying it to the SWAT outside of the home, so they know how irate he's becoming by the second, with escalating aggression. "Tim please stop it, you're scaring the shit out of me and Brianna! Just give yourself up, we'll still be there for you". Loraine said, wanting him to turn himself in. As a loving wife, she would honor her vows, loving him and being by his side while he's in jail for better or for worse. Right now she just wants him to stop terrifying her and their daughter. "Are they telling you to say that stupid shit! I know how this thing works!" Detective Ritter snapped thinking the SWAT negotiators are telling Loraine this to calm him. Suddenly, shifting his attention, he heard the back door being aggressively breached, his head turned quick towards the loud sound, followed by the front door being rammed in. At the same time the SWAT shot a concussion grenade inside the living room window sounding off loud like a explosion, to disorient Detective Ritter. He pulled it together, aware this would come, so he fired multiple rounds in each direction before thrusting his foot into the bedroom door, forcing it open, wanting to end it all, taking his wife and daughter with him.

Especially feeling like he failed them beyond repair. As he entered the bedroom, SWAT moved through the house wanting to save Loraine and Brianna. Unexpectedly she brought into view a 9mm Sig, her husband purchased for her years ago for protection when he's not home. Loraine's conflicted mentally and emotionally, taking aim sliding her finger inside of the trigger guard. Milliseconds passing, she's torn between killing her husband, the father of her daughter. At the same time he's raising his gun to take aim at her and Brianna, which she's shielding her daughter instinctively. Her heart is thumping, her mind his overwhelmed with thoughts, as she found the trigger. Then it happened. Tim Ritter's body lift off the floor being thrust backwards with force, from a high powered sniper rifle round that went through the window into his chest, almost cutting him in half. He was dead before he hit the floor, with all of his internal organs being blown out of his back. Loraine still pointing her gun unaware he's not getting back up. The SWAT sniper radioing in to the other team members. "Suspect down, all is secured". The team inside of the house closed in on the bedroom seeing the shocked and traumatized Loraine still gripping her weapon starring intently straight ahead like Tim is still standing in front of her. "Ma'am, everything is going to be okay now. Can you please lower the weapon?" The SWAT member asked as he moved in slow, coming over to her, seeing she's in shock by this mentally and emotionally tormenting situation. He removed her weapon before continuing on speaking. "You're safe now, come with us ma'am. You may want to cover your daughter's eyes as you exit the room". He said knowing it is too graphic for a child to see, let alone it being her father. She did as instructed, with tears streaming down her face, stepping over her husband's lifeless body. If Tim would've been patient he would've known Wilson's scheduled to leave the hospital today.

Chapter 22

On the other side of the bridge in Harrisburg, Red Rain was on the Hillside of the city, hollering at this nigga Bundles that just came home after giving a Life bid back for a body. He's now forty years old, slim built, dark skinned nigga, that's hungry to get what belongs to him, after being locked down for so long. Bundles is also a original YG gang member. Now the young teenage niggas hold down the brand putting in work, thanks to the other original members Guru and Duttaman. Bundles came to grab four bricks from Red Rain, since him and his team was breaking this shit down to eight balls, quarters and half's. "It's the first of the month, my team going blow through this in a few days and I'll be getting back to you". Buddle's said, passing the bag with the bricks to Duttaman. Duttaman a real street nigga and shooter, having done a bid himself for putting in work doing drive bys and walk bys, not giving a fuck, especially having the war ready mindset, always totting two black steel snub nose .357magnums. He loves these weapons because they're more powerful, reliable and accurate than a automatic, not having to worry about shit jamming up or having to chamber a round. Duttaman standing six foot one, brown skin, medium built, mustache, light goatee, low hair cut, no waves, no shape up, he on some rough grinding hard shit right now. "I got whatever you need, no matter what time of the month it is. You got the paper I have the raw grade A". Red Rain said flipping through the bag of money, making sure the count is right. "Is the paper good beautiful?" Bundles asked. "Yeah it's official". "Now off the business side of things, and more onto you side of things". Bundles said looking on at Red Rain in her dark red body hugging jeans, displaying her curves sculpted to perfection. The white T-shirt cut off exposing her flat stomach. The T-shirt having red glitter print that reads: DON'T TEASE ME! Topping it off the tan suede stiletto boots, boosting her ass up.

Red Rain smiling having lured majority of her clientele in through her Instagram account, being a social media influencer. She mislead them, weeding out the real hustlas that's focused on getting money, not just the ones who think they can hit it because they flipping ounces. Her main focus is business right now. Besides if she want sex she has TK and Suga Baby for that. "You ain't ready for all of this, especially having four kilos to off load for the first of the month". She said tossing his words back at him to see how focus and hungry he is. "This raw coke going move itself, leaving me plenty of time to focus on

The Crown Is Mine

all of that ass you hear me". Bundle said taking in all of her exotic beauty. "Now why would I want to fuck a nigga that's not focused on his paper?" She fired back making Duttaman laugh until Bundles looked over at him. "That shit ain't funny. You a tease and you wearing that shirt talking about don't tease. All that ass and you playing with a nigga. Better be glad you the plug, or I would block you on the gram for that stupid shit". He said turning to exit with Duttaman. She walked them to the door letting them out. Duttaman tossed the peace sign up. Bundles turned looking at her shaking his head, yet still wanting to smash, but it is what it is. She shut the door locking it before calling up Suga Baby on the video chat. Her face appeared looking sexy, having a glow like her and TK was fucking. "What's up you sexy beast?" Suga Baby said getting excited seeing her girlfriend. "Everything is coming to an end up this way. I should be home soon. I can't wait, you know how I get when I'm away from y'all. Me and my body be missing the excitement and love I get from y'all". Red Rain, expressed really embracing this bond they share. "If you really miss me, I can sneak up that way to treat you and your body the way you like it, making it rain in the bed". Suga Baby said being funny and sensual. "More like a flood with your tongue, talent and finger magic". Red Rain said with a big smile, allowing images of it all to enter her mind, having Suga Baby here with her. "For real, you can't come this way, it's too risky". She added. "Wishful thinking to let you know I care. Now onto the other side of things. You coming this way to take care of that, or we sending someone your way?" Suga Baby asked focusing back to business of money and power. Also to show La Vieja that they're capable of handling this much product and power she placed on them. Before she could respond to her about business, a knock came across her door. "Hold up babe, I know these fools ain't come back?" She said walking to the door. Suddenly, the front door flew open abruptly from a foot thrusting into it. She seen Latinos forcing their way in. She turned just as fast trying to get her gun off of the couch, until a round was fired hitting her in the hamstring dropping her. Red Rain hitting the floor turning over facing guns aimed at her, so she turned the phone allowing Suga Baby to see what's going on. It's five Latinos surrounding Red Rain with guns. "Nooooo!" Suga Baby screamed seeing their guns aimed at her. "Don't kill her!" She pleaded, unaware these goons are Latin Kings connected to La Reina a Latin Queen. After La Reina's murder they watched the city and state for a sudden influx of product, that determined who wanted her dead taking over as she once had the power and position to do so. The goons halted squeezing on Red Rain hearing Suga Baby's screaming voice. The leader of this crew Flaco, looking at Suga Baby on the screen. "I known your face from being wanted. Are you

The Crown Is Mine

the one responsible for killing La Reina?" Flaco said staring at her almost as if he could kill her through the screen. "No". She lied vehemently, thinking it would be suffice, for him. "Then it's this one on the floor". Flaco said taking aim at Red Rain, ready to kill her in exchange for the blood that was shed, in killing La Reina. "It was me!" Suga Baby blurted out against her better judgement. At the same time wanting to save Red Rain by any means. "Please don't kill her, she didn't know anything about it". Suga Baby pleaded, heartbroken with her eyes becoming glassy in fear of losing this person she's emotionally attached to. "Don't beg for my life baby. I love you. Whatever happens fuck it. It's a part of this lifestyle". Red Rain said not wanting Suga Baby to show any sign of weakness, also feeling the end coming. "Que le pasa a ella?" The goon asked what is wrong with her, meaning Red Rain standing firm. Something they didn't expect with her exotic beauty. "You kill one of ours, we kill all of yours". The skinny Latin King member name Flaco said. "You can take my life for hers, plus I'll give you a million dollars". Suga Baby said, at the same time, TK came rushing into the bedroom with his gun out, having heard her screaming when he was downstairs lifting weights in the garage. She pointed at the screen. He came around into the view, seeing the Spanish nigga with the tear drop tattoos on his face, only having a mustache, a king's crown on his neck, visible with a lion staring intently. "Hermano you must be the puta that assisted in killing La Reina?" Flaco said, not for sure, having heard from his street sources it was a male and female that took out La Reina and her security. "Babe they shot Rain. It's five of them having her at gun point". Suga Baby said. Hearing this shifting TK's demeanor to gangsta mode to protect what he loves, including his position of power. "This don't end well for you, if you bring harm to her. The people you want is right here. You can come to us or we'll come find you". TK said firmly. "Es muy tarde Hermano". Flaco said making TK aware it's too late. He looked over at his gang brother preparing to give the nod to execute her, making a statement to anyone that fucks with the Latin Kings. Then it happened. The roaring of magnums sounding off, coming from Duttaman's .357mganums. Slugs crashing into the chest of the two goons closest to Red Rain, thrusting them back away from her, then he shift his guns, one at Flaco and his associate. Red Rain pulling herself up quick, ignoring the pain of the bullet in her leg, as she grabbed her gun off the couch. "I forgot my phone. Lucky for you huh?" Duttaman said seeing his phone on the end of the coffee table. "You want me to kill this nigga and his bitch ass gang friends or what?" Duttaman asked. Red Rain now standing up snatching her phone back from Flaco. "I'm okay now baby. Should I leave this mutha fucka and his friends?" Red Rain asked TK as she took Flaco's gun.

Duttaman did the same, taking the other Latin King goon's guns. TK knowing these mutha fuckas would come back stronger if they kill them especially with them finding out who Red Rain is, it's inevitable. "Send these Spanish niggas a message they can understand baby girl". TK responded. She lowered her gun shooting Flaco in the stomach thrusting him back, knocking the wind out of him. "Ahi Dios Mio! Cabrona!" Flaco yelled out feeling the pain. "That's for shooting me in my leg mutha fucka! If you or these bitch ass mutha fuckas come at me again, you better aim for the head or you and all you love will be dead! Now get the fuck out of my crib!" Red Rain stated firmly. Duttaman went over to the two unconscious goons he shot, smacking them across the face with his gun awaking them, to feel the pain of the slugs that slammed into their upper body. "Get up nigga, this shit is real huh? Now get the fuck up before the next slug leave you sleep for real nigga". Duttaman said staring at these Spanish niggas grabbing the area he shot them, as they walk towards the door picking up Flaco who is hit the worse, helping him out of the house. Duttaman came over to Red Rain. " You got to relocate, this spot is burned with these crazy mutha fuckas trying to get at you". Duttaman said. "Good looking folk".

Red Rain said limping over to secure the money she got from Bundles. She didn't have clothes here, this spot she rented was strictly to conduct business. She didn't even have product here. That was stashed at another location. Duttaman man helped her down the steps over to her car. "You need anything else, get at us. You know how we ride". Duttaman said. "I appreciate you forgetting your phone". She said being funny and real at the same time, realizing how close she was to the end. He laughed getting into the car within Bundles, putting him down with the crazy shit. Red Rain still clutching her phone with TK and Suga Baby still tuned in, making sure she is safe. "You good or do you need me to fly that way?" TK asked. "Nah you don't have to come. I'm a hit the hospital get this bullet out of my leg, then fly down tonight". Red Rain said. She has to leave the city for a little to regroup, so she can be a hundred percent to hold shit down, especially with letting the Latin King goons live. They're bound to come back wanting to avenge their Queen Tiara 'La Reina' Rodrigez. "From now on you need to have a team around you at all times, when you moving around up there". TK said never wanting her to be compromised like this again. It put him and Suga Baby in a helpless position. "Hurry back home bitch, I can't afford to be losing my mind thinking you was about to be taken away from us". Suga Baby said. Red Rain warmed by her words and sincere concern. "I love y'all too". She responded, blowing them a kiss before ending the call, as she drove to the hospital to take care if her leg.

The Crown Is Mine

Chapter 23

Down Atlanta Trappa-D is pulling up in the hood with his new hunter green Dodge Durango, sitting on 26 inch chrome rims, light green tint, white leather seats piped in hunter green, flowing with the exterior custom paint. He also has two thirteen inch TVs that fold down in the back for the passenger's entertainment, along with game consoles and system. Trappa-D having his way looking the part of a hood boss, feeling himself. The young bucks of the hood he kept with him, all younger than fifteen looking up to Trappa-D. They also in the truck with him as he pulled up in the hood, coming from balling out at the mall, shopping with the little hommies. Little Ki Ki coming out of the lay low spot, seeing Trappa-D in this new whip with the hommies. Each of them bopping their heads to the music, listening to 2Sauce remix By Sleepy Hallow featuring Skillibeng. The young bucks hopped out of the truck with their bags of clothing and sneakers they grabbed at the mall thanks to the big hommie Trappa-D who splurged on them, giving each of them motivation to get to this paper, while looking the part. Little Ki Ki shaking her head as she approached the truck. "Say man you doing too much ya feel me?" Little Ki Ki said adjusting her Nike baseball cap to the right. "None of us got jobs and you drawing attention to what we should be doing on the low fool". She added being focused having stacked her money, not worried about stunting or being flashy. Little Ki Ki having done research on her out and endgame with real estate, buying land and property to secure her future and finances. " What you want me to do shawty? I ain't taking these clothes or my whip back". Trappa-D said puffing the blunt of purple haze, blowing out a cloud of smoke, showing gold fronts iced out. "Be a leader by showing these niggas how to get and save they paper, instead of blowing it on shit that ain't going to be worth shit ya feel me". As Little Ki Ki was talking the little hommies went to put their clothes and sneakers in the crib. They knew they had to get back out on the block to chase this paper, especially after the get money talk Trappa-D gave them at the mall and on the way back to the hood, pumping them up. "Aye Ki Ki, you my hommie from day one shawty. If it wasn't you, I wouldn't pay you no mind ya feel me, but I got love and respect for ya G, so I'm a tone it down. I know you got my back even if I don't see it right in the moment". Trappa-D said acknowledging what she pointed out to him. Little Ki Ki's phone started ringing shifting her attention, knowing the ring tone is her girlfriend and ex-stripper Karin 'Babycakes' Lin, a exotic Korean-Afro-American standing five foot six, a sculpted body with curves, plump ass with injections, small waist line, 36D breast, full lips making her look like a million dollar Asian Barbie. Grey sparkling eyes, a luring smile with dimples, perfect white teeth, silky long jet black hair reaching the middle of her back, when she lets it down. Karin is twenty five years old, not looking a day over nineteen. She danced her way through college, before securing her degree in marketing, business that lead to other ventures working for VproMarketing.com before starting her own real estate business, that is now seeing a increase in income, thanks to her girlfriend Little Ki Ki. "What's up Babycakes?" "I was calling to let you know I found a building with a store front that has apartments above. I think it would be a good investment, if you're open to it?" "Send me pics, if I like what I see, then we can check it out together". Little Ki Ki responded. "Okay I'll send them now". Karin said doing just that, along with a picture of her in a powder blue lingerie looking into the camera with seductive eyes. Little Ki Ki checking the pictures of the property, then coming across the photo of Babycakes. Little Ki Ki gave a brief smile. "Yeah I like what I see. It's worth investing in to". " Mmmh, me or the property?"

"Both, but I have shit to take care of out here, to secure taking care of you and the investment". Little Ki

Ki responded staying focus on the grind. "I love you and what you mean to what we have together". Karin said in a soft sensual tone. Karin is the only one that warms Little Ki Ki's heart. "Yeah, I love me too. I'll see you tonight, to show you how I feel about you Babycakes". She said ending the call. Trappa-D watching how she managed business and her chick all at the same time. "You making moves on the low huh?" Trappa-D asked hearing the real estate talk. "When you really ready, I'll put you down with this, so you can have something to fall back on ya feel me. Right now we need to get the little hommies focused so they don't think this shit is all about sneakers and Gucci". Little Ki Ki said, at the same time gunfire at the top of the block erupted, shifting both of their attention, they reached for their guns. Trappa-D looking in the rearview mirror as Little Ki Ki started walking fast in that direction seeing it's someone from their squad doing the shooting. Trappa-D jumped out of the truck catching up to Little Ki Ki. "What's wrong with these fools?" She asked seeing the little nigga Dre has shot a crack head. "Yo nigga what you shooting fiends fo?" Trappa-D asked Dre since be brought him into the clique. "Say man this fool tried to switch me out and run. So I bust a cap in his ass". Dre responded showing Trappa-D the switched bag, that's not the same color or quality of their product. Dre only fourteen with braids, brown skin, skinny not taking no shit. "If that nigga dead

The Crown Is Mine

it's going to fuck up our paper around here and we don't need that ya feel me?" Little Ki Ki said. "He ain't dead I shot him in the ass I told ya". Dre responded kicking the fiend in the side, " Get up fool for I shoot you again". The fiend opened his eyes wide turning over putting his hands up. "Aye man don't kill me, I just wanted to get high, and y'all got that good shit, that have my heart thumping and chasing for more". "Stupid nigga get the fuck up out of here". Little Ki Ki snapped angered by this situation, not wanting anything or anyone to halt this flow of cash or good thing they have going out here. Dre followed the fiend pushing him down the block. "You thought shit was sweet out here huh? You better be glad I didn't hit you with a head shot, cause getting high wouldn't be on ya mind then fool". Dre said pressing his gun in the fiend's back daring him to try some stupid shit. " Now get the fuck out of here you dumb nigga". "Can I get a rock for the pain in my ass nigga, that shit hurt, plus I ain't going tell". Dre gave him a dime of crack, buying his silence, all because the fiend wants to get high. He probably won't even go to the hospital. "Don't come back around here no mo". Dre said, watching the crack head limp away fast, keep looking back in fear he's going to be shot again. Little Ki Ki looking at Trappa-D knowing they have to pull the block together, running a more organized operation, with no weak or loose ends. "We have to groom these little niggas to focus on the money and not shit that takes them away from it". Little Ki Ki said walking back to the crib with Trappa-D to have a sit down conversation to plant a seed in his mind too, with all of the product they have coming in, that demands focus, with no interruptions, or unnecessary attention from the law, that could side track their plans or halt the growth in this drug game. Any mistakes or losing focus could be the demise of the game and or your life. Little Ki Ki expressed to Trappa-D, wanting him to be tuned in, instead of always turning up.

Chapter 24

Back up north, Red Rain is finishing up getting her leg wound patched up. The nurse giving her the all clear to leave. She was questioned by the cops when she first came to the hospital. She told them it was a drive by and she got caught in the crossfire. With all of the daily shootings they didn't question her further, assuming she didn't know who shot her. As she's leaving, limping through the hall, she was passing a room hearing loud Spanish speaking getting her attention. She look, seeing that it's a room of Latin Kings, some are the ones they let go, the other is Flaco the one she shot in the stomach. They were talking to a stocky bald bead Latino with gang tattoos all over his face, showing how many bodies he got, and his rank as a sanctioned gang member. She also noticed the crown on his neck. Her heart rate picking up, just as her pace walking as fast as she could away from these crazy mutha fuckas. She didn't want to have another run in with them. She only wanted to go home and be next to TK and Suga Baby. She walk pass the nurse's station seeing two police officers being jovial with the ladies. Red Rain now heading towards the elevator texting Suga Baby. Red Rain: Patched up coming home 2U. Suga Baby: Hurry! Can't wait! Red Rain: OK luv U Suga Baby: We luv U2 After reading the text she pressed the button to get the elevator to the floor she's on. Thoughts of how shit went down at the crib running through her mind, knowing Duttaman saved her, so she owe the YG hommies for his timing. As these thoughts are going through her mind, she can hear the police radios approaching. She glanced over her shoulder seeing it's the two officers that was at the nurse's station, talking about which one each other likes. The elevator chimed signifying the door is about to open. The doors slid open revealing two Latin King members, one of them Duttaman didn't shoot allowing him to leave with the others. He noticed Red Rain instantly. Her heart seeming to leap into her chest as her mind is processing a out at lightening speed, seeing this crazy mutha fuckas in front of her reaching for his gun, even with the presence of the two cops behind her. Unlike Red Rain these gang members are always strapped. She left her gun in the car not wanting to get caught up with it in here. Without hesitation the other Latin King followed suit reaching for his gun seeing shit is about to pop off. With the surge of adrenaline rushing through her body, she ignored the pain in her thigh, turning quick towards the officers running in between them. Her sudden movement alerting them to the immediate

The Crown Is Mine

threat in front of them, forcing them to react fast removing their side arms. Red Rain ran between them as the officers took aim at the gang related goons. Abrupt roaring of gunfire sounding off throughout the hospital, displaying the level of determination of these two gang members wanting to kill Red Rain for the shit she did earlier disrespecting the crown of being a Latin King. The officers got one of the gang members, but not before the other caught the officer in the face twisting his head, snapping his neck, with his brains ejected out the other side. The other Latin King hit the elevator button closing the door to make his escape. The other radioing in "Officer down! Shots fired officer down!" He yelled over the radio giving his location so other units can respond, along with hospital security. The goon in the elevator taking his phone out calling the hommie in the room with Flaco. They too heard the barrage of gunfire, placing them on high alert protecting their gang brother laying wounded in the bed. "Oye that puta that shot Flaco is on your floor. I tried to kill her, but the cops jumped in. I killed that cabron too". Tito said pumped up, looking on at his slumped hommie with slugs in his body and face. "Paco Es muerte bro". Tito added. "Don't let that cabrona get out of here". Don Rico said a angered by this taking place.

Don Rico is a high ranking Latin King, controlling all in Pennsylvania, being the one sanctioning all hits and money movement to be sent back to the home country. He is also seeking revenge and blood for the person responsible for killing La Reina, because she's one of their own that brought a lot of money that helped the organization out with securing guns, product, soldiers and resources. Red Rain taking the fire exit stairs, rushing down each step ignoring the pain in her leg, in fear of getting caught, tortured or killed by these crazy mutha fuckas, that don't have any regard for life or respect for officers of the law, making them extremely dangerous. Soon as she closed in on the second floor, preparing to go to the ground floor. The first floor door popped open, followed by the fifth floor door where she started her descent. She pressed up against the wall, holding her breath to keep silent. "You see that bitch?" Don Rico yelled out from the fifth floor, down to Tito who is looking up at him from the ground floor. "Nothing bro, she probably still up there". Tito said since he didn't see her. "Stay by the door in case she comes from another floor. Don't fuck this up!" Don Rico stated firmly. Red Rain can hear the door upstairs closing, followed by the door on the first floor. She exhaled slowly, taking steps towards the railing, looking up and down. Nothing. They're both gone She didn't want to risk heading to the first floor, so she tried to open the second floor door. Nothing, it didn't open. Why? She questioned looking at the door. It's a children's ward, so they have to secure it to protect the vulnerable children from the kidnappers, pedophiles and other predators. She walk down to the first floor walking up on the door slowly peeping through the window, seeing Tito looking around as he's walking away. Red Rain looked to the right seeing the reason, it's cops coming in response to the officer down call over the radio.

Soon as she came out multiple uniformed cops flood the first floor, sweeping the hospital for the description given of the Latino gang member. The other officers rushing to the fifth floor, where the downed officer is. She hurried calling TK not wanting to worry Suga Baby too much, especially after she loss her shit earlier, thinking Red Rain was about to be taken from her. "What's good baby girl?!" TK asked. "These Latin King fools done loss they fucking mind, trying to get at me inside of the hospital". She responded, looking at the anger in his face. TK wishing he was present to protect her. "Them bitch ass mutha fuckas don't what no real smoke. I'll bury all of them bitches, if they hurt you". TK vented. Red Rain making it to her S600L Mercedes Benz starting the car, when a black Honda Accord pulled in front of her car blocking her in. "These niggas just blocked me in!" Red Rain yelled out, reaching for her gun behind the passenger seat. The four goons exited the Honda quick aiming their guns at Red Rain. Tito came running from the side of the hospital over to the car with his gun out, his cell phone in the other hand talking to Don Rico. "Espera un minuto! Don Rico wants her alive!" Tito yelled out. Red Rain hearing this relayed it to TK. "Babe they want me alive this mutha fucka said. I'm thinking, I end this shit now taking as many of them out that I can". She said feeling cornered, not wanting to be taken alive to be tortured, then killed. They couldn't see Red Rain behind the dark tint, they only knew that she just got inside of the car. They still had their weapons aimed at the drivers side window. "I can't agree with that decision, because Suga Baby would never forgive me for that. They want you alive only means they're looking for a exchange. We'll come for you at any cost, blood, bodies or money, we won't leave you stranded with these stupid mutha fuckas". TK said. The gang member came to the door tapping on the window with his gun.

"Abre la puerta puta!" He told her to open the door. She looked down at her gun then back up at the other Latinos, weighing her options, in taking out as many as she can. Also conflicted, holding onto the hope of being reunited with Suga Baby and TK. Being in their presence again, feeling the warm of their bodies next to hers, along with the affection that comes with it. "TK, I love you and Suga Baby with all my heart". She said expressing what she feels, not knowing if she'll ever see them again, even if TK promised to come for her, she don't know how long these gang members are willing to keep her around before sending a message not to fuck with the Latin Kings, killing her off. TK gritting his teeth watching this unfold, seeing the look in Red Rain's eyes, being in this compromising position. He's even more pissed off wishing he could be there to protect and hold her down, killing all of these bitch ass Latin King niggas, for disrespecting his ride or die bitch. She opened the door, gun still in her lap, one hand on it, until the goon put his gun to her head. "You die now if you raise that gun up!" He said in a aggressive tone, reaching in taking it from her. "Now get the fuck out of the car!" He added, the others came over quick snatching her up, rushing over to the back of the Honda, jamming her inside, with their guns pressing up against her, in case she thought about getting crazy, fighting with them in attempt to break free. The Latin King soldiers didn't care about who she is, her exotic beauty or her position in the drug game. They only followed orders from Don Rico to handle this business by any means, and they did just that. Nothing or no one else at this point even matters.

GOOD 2 GO PUBLISHING CATALOG ORDER FORM

To order books, please fill out the order form below (Please allow up to 2 weeks for shipping)
Make checks payable to: Good2Go Publishing P.O Box 758, Laveen, AZ 85339

Name: _____ Address: _____ City: _____

State: _____ Zip Code: _____ Phone: _____ Email:

Item Name	Price	Qty	Amnt
48 Hours to Die – Silk White	$15.00		
A Hustler's Dream – Ernest Morris	$15.00		
A Hustler's Dream 2 – Ernest Morris	$15.00		
A Thug's Devotion – J.L. Rose	$15.00		
Affliction – Assa Raymond Baker	$15.00		
Affliction 2 – Assa Raymond Baker	$15.00		
All Eyes on Gunz – Warren Holloway	$15.00		
All Eyes on Gunz 2 – Warren Holloway	$15.00		
All Eyes on Gunz 3 – Warren Holloway	$15.00		
All Eyes on Gunz 4 – Warren Holloway	$15.00		
Betrayal Within – Ernest Morris	$15.00		
Black Reign – Ernest Morris	$15.00		
Bloody Mayhem Down South – Trayvon Jackson	$15.00		
Bloody Mayhem Down South 2 – Trayvon Jackson	$15.00		
Business Is Business – Silk White	$15.00		
Business Is Business 2 – Silk White	$15.00		
Business Is Business 3 – Silk White	$15.00		
Cash In Cash Out – Assa Raymond Baker	$15.00		
Cash In Cash Out 2 – Assa Raymond Baker	$15.00		
Chi City Boyz – Asia Hill	$15.00		
Childhood Sweethearts – Jacob Spears	$15.00		
Childhood Sweethearts 2 – Jacob Spears	$15.00		
Childhood Sweethearts 3 – Jacob Spears	$15.00		
Childhood Sweethearts 4 – Jacob Spears	$15.00		
Connected To The Plug – Dwan Williams	$15.00		
Connected To The Plug 2 – Dwan Williams	$15.00		
Connected To The Plug 3 – Dwan Williams	$15.00		
Connected To The Plug 4 – Dwan Williams	$15.00		
Connected to the Plug 4 – Dwan Williams	$15.00		
Cost of Betrayal – Warren Holloway	$15.00		
Cost of Betrayal 2 – Warren Holloway	$15.00		
Death by Association – Ernest Morris	$15.00		
Death by Association 2 – Ernest Morris	$15.00		
Dreams Life – Assa Raymond Baker	$15.00		
Dreams Life 2 – Assa Raymond Baker	$15.00		
Flipping Numbers – Ernest Morris	$15.00		
Flipping Numbers 2 – Ernest Morris	$15.00		
Forbidden Pleasure – Ernest Morris	$15.00		
He Loves Me, He Loves You Not – Mychea	$15.00		
He Loves Me, He Loves You Not 2 – Mychea	$15.00		
He Loves Me, He Loves You Not 3 – Mychea	$15.00		
He Loves Me, He Loves You Not 4 – Mychea	$15.00		
He Loves Me, He Loves You Not 5 – Mychea	$15.00		
Healing In The Midst of Adversity –Michelle Murray	$15.00		
Killing Signs – Ernest Morris	$15.00		
Killing Signs 2 – Ernest Morris	$15.00		
King of the Night – Warren Holloway	$15.00		
Kings of the Block – Dwan Williams	$15.00		
Kings of the Block 2 – Dwan Williams	$15.00		
Lord of My Land – J.M. Morrison	$15.00		
Lost and Turned Out – Ernest Morris	$15.00		
Love and Basketball – J.L. Rose	$15.00		
Love and Deception – Warren Holloway	$15.00		
Love Hates Violence – De'Wayne Maris	$15.00		
Love Hates Violence 2 – De'Wayne Maris	$15.00		
Love Hates Violence 3 – De'Wayne Maris	$15.00		
Love Hates Violence 4 – De'Wayne Maris	$15.00		
Loyalty to a Gangsta – J.L. Rose	$15.00		
Married To Da Streets – Silk White	$15.00		
Mercenary in Love – J.L. Rose	$15.00		
Mercenary in Love 2 – J.L. Rose	$15.00		
My Besties – Asia Hill	$15.00		
My Besties 2 – Asia Hill	$15.00		
My Besties 3 – Asia Hill	$15.00		
My Besties 4 – Asia Hill	$15.00		
My Boyfriend's Wife – Mychea	$15.00		
My Boyfriend's Wife 2 – Mychea	$15.00		
My Brothers Envy – J. L. Rose	$15.00		
My Brothers Envy 2 – J. L. Rose	$15.00		

Item Name	Price	Qty	Amnt
My Brothers Envy 3 – J. L. Rose	$15.00		
Naughty Housewives – Ernest Morris	$15.00		
Naughty Housewives 2 – Ernest Morris	$15.00		
Naughty Housewives 3 – Ernest Morris	$15.00		
Naughty Housewives 4 – Ernest Morris	$15.00		
Never Be The Same – Silk White	$15.00		
Scarred Knuckles – Raymond Baker	$15.00		
Scarred Knuckles 2 – Raymond Baker	$15.00		
Secrets in the Dark Ernest Morris	$15.00		
Shades of Revenge – Assa Raymond Baker	$15.00		
Shoebox Money – Warren Holloway	$15.00		
Slumped – Jason Brent	$15.00		
Someone's Gonna Get It – Mychea	$15.00		
Stranded – Silk White	$15.00		
Supreme & Justice – Ernest Morris	$15.00		
Supreme & Justice 2 – Ernest Morris	$15.00		
Supreme & Justice 3 – Ernest Morris	$15.00		
Sweet Peas Tough Choices – Silk White	$15.00		
Tears of a Hustler – Silk White	$15.00		
Tears of a Hustler 2 – Silk White	$15.00		
Tears of a Hustler 3 – Silk White	$15.00		
Tears of a Hustler 4– Silk White	$15.00		
Tears of a Hustler 5 – Silk White	$15.00		
Tears of a Hustler 6 – Silk White	$15.00		
The Excitement I Bring – Warren Holloway	$15.00		
The Excitement I Bring 2 – Warren Holloway	$15.00		
The Last Love Letter – Warren Holloway	$15.00		
The Last Love Letter 2 – Warren Holloway	$15.00		
The Panty Ripper – Reality Way	$15.00		
The Panty Ripper 3 – Reality Way	$15.00		
The Serial Cheater – Silk White	$15.00		
The Solution – J. M. Morrison	$15.00		
The Teflon Queen – Silk White	$15.00		
The Teflon Queen 2 – Silk White	$15.00		
The Teflon Queen 3 – Silk White	$15.00		
The Teflon Queen 4 – Silk White	$15.00		
The Teflon Queen 5 – Silk White	$15.00		
The Teflon Queen 6 – Silk White	$15.00		
The Vacation – Silk White	$15.00		
Tied to a Boss – J. L. Rose	$15.00		
Tied to a Boss 2 – J. L. Rose	$15.00		
Tied to a Boss 3 – J. L. Rose	$15.00		
Tied to a Boss 4 – J. L. Rose	$15.00		
Tied to a Boss 5 – J. L. Rose	$15.00		
Time Is Money – Silk White	$15.00		
Tomorrow's Not Promised – Robert Torres	$15.00		
Tomorrow's Not Promised 2 – Robert Torres	$15.00		
Trapped in Love – Ernest Morris	$15.00		
Two Mask One Heart – Jacob Spears & Trayvon Jackson	$15.00		
Two Mask One Heart 2 – Jacob Spears & Trayvon Jackson	$15.00		
Two Mask One Heart 3 – Jacob Spears & Trayvon Jackson	$15.00		
Wife – Raneissa Baker	$15.00		
Wife 2 – Raneissa Baker	$15.00		
Wrong Place Wrong Time – Silk White	$15.00		
Young Goonz – Reality Way	$15.00		
Secrets in the Dark 2 – Ernest Morris (New Release)	$15.00		
Secrets in the Dark 1 – Ernest Morris (New release)	$15.00		
The Danger That Lurks Within – Ernest Morris	$15.00		
When Love Happens – Warren Holloway	$15.00		
The Unexpected – Warren	$15.00		
Finding Her Love – Warren Holloway	$15.00		
Murder and Deception – Warren Holloway	$15.00		
Entanglement – Raymond Baker	$15.00		
The Crown Is Mine. Part I	$15.00		
The Crown Is Mine. Part II	$15.00		
The Crown Is Mine. Part III	$15.00		

NOTE: Please make sure the books you order are accepted we are not responsible for rejected orders.

Total: Shipping (Free) Us Media Mail